Red Strings Attached

Lainey Schmidt

 iUniverse®

RED STRINGS ATTACHED

iUniverse books may be ordered through booksellers or by contacting:

iUniverse
1663 Liberty Drive
Bloomington, IN 47403
www.iuniverse.com
1-800-Authors (1-800-288-4677)

ISBN: 978-1-5320-9675-4 (sc)
ISBN: 978-1-5320-9676-1 (e)

Library of Congress Control Number: 2020904201

Print information available on the last page.

iUniverse rev. date: 03/10/2020

Prologue

I've never liked the color red. I despise it really. I avoid it at every opportunity unless it's perfectly polished nails or a matte lipstick. When I caught an article online about love that followed suit to the cliché, big-red-heart, mushy love jargon, I almost lost interest. I wish it were called the blue, orange, or even green string theory. The red string theory has consumed my view on love. After my interest was piqued, I turned to multiple sites for additional information. It was rare for me to want to dive in deeper on a mini article intended for likes and shares, but I related to it and knew it would add clarity to where I was with past and current relationships. I should have been preparing for the long day of work ahead of me the following day, but with wine in one hand and my dog flopped over one of my legs as my husband read a book beside me under lamplight, I knew I wasn't getting up anytime soon, so I thought, *What the heck?* and dove in.

It is said that we are all born with a red string attached to our pinky finger on one end and to our soulmate's thumb at the other end. No matter how life twists and tangles the thread, it will never break. The theory has been passed down through generations and cultures and has been reworded in many ways to fit its relative niche. My favorite version is that we all have two red strings, one attached at each pinky. Just as we have a devil over one shoulder and an angel over the other, we have equally contradicting loves on either finger. We may fall in love many times in a lifetime, but only twice will we experience genuine love—our most true-to-the-core loves. It doesn't matter what decisions you make in your life or the paths you choose, how you meet someone, or if that person seems like the *one* in the moment. You'll meet the when-you-know-you-know kind of love, and if you're really lucky, you'll meet your two red strings. I met both within two years—the most insane, unbelievable two years I've lived yet. I learned a lot about myself and what I'm capable of during this time. This rare, invaluable lesson included heart strain, ache, and break, but most importantly, great life changes that I wouldn't trade for anything.

One string connects you to your passionate love. This love is the gasoline to your fire—hot, intense, and chaotic. You drive each other crazy, to the point where you feel you're at the cusp of insanity, but you can't get enough of it. You're happy in your craziness. You can't be without each other. When you are, you itch to reconnect. You raise each other's blood pressure. You'll argue and fight, but you'll never leave. If you ever consider breaking up, you're pulled back together like magnets. It's the love that Frida Kahlo and Diego are said to have had together. It's love, it's hate, it's passion, it's even romantic, and there's enough fuel in your tank to keep this beautiful fire burning for a lifetime.

Then you have your peaceful red string. This string is connected to a love that is calm, effortless and just feels natural, like your body and mind could do it on autopilot. In this love, you are each other's motivator, you bring out the best in each other, the love is pure and true. It's full of trust and care and the kind of passion that makes you love every second of just being in each other's presence. You could live without each other, but you'd never want to.

These two are your "people," the ones on this planet for you. Even when you think you've burned bridges or disconnected yourself; this person is always there. The strings cannot be separated, and your bonds cannot be broken. There are many people in the world who will never meet their red-string loves and some who won't act on the feelings they get when they do meet their people. The guarantee in the theory is that your decisions in life won't dissolve your threads. It doesn't guarantee that you won't be too shy, stubborn, or scared to act on it. Did you feel your chest vibrate when the barista touched your hand by accident? Do you go into the same spot in the library to study because you know the guy with the glasses will be at his usual spot as well? It might just be lust, or it might just be one of the greatest loves of your life.

Another theory that I cannot get behind is when they say that time heals *all* wounds. I call BS on that one. Physically, yes, science has proven the body will regenerate itself every seven years. Bruises will heal, scars will fade, and bones will mend. However, the mind is an exception to this rule. Our bodies can forget about it during this so called "regeneration period". Its well-being is irrelevant to time. For the mind's heart—the one that aches at the sound of someone's name, a memory, or the realization of their absence, that one is unrepairable—time doesn't stand a chance. The mind's heart makes decision making in relationships almost impossible, it's what blinds us to who we've become when we give someone all of us without looking back to see how we've changed. It will wreck us and never skip a beat—especially those of us who are suckers for love, the ones who think life might just turn out like a movie or a good country love song if we hope for it hard enough. That's me, and I'm not ashamed to admit it. It's gotten the best of me in the past and will continue to in the future. I melt at the end of every romance film or at the climax of a good book, and don't even get me started on weddings. Tissues please! When the bride and groom exchange vows and promise to be there for each other through the thick and the thin, the good and the bad, you would think my dog died in that very moment because of my incoherent sobbing. Even as a plus-one to a wedding of a friend's friend, the wedding of a couple I don't personally know, I'm crying through most of the ceremony. At the age of five, when everyone's favorite mermaid sailed off on her ship happily married to her earthbound prince, I sobbed. My parents couldn't figure out why I would cry at the end of this movie every time I watched it until the reason behind the repetition shined through. They should have shipped me off to boarding school then. When it became my turn to try out love, I walked up eager and doomed with my heart in hand.

1

Take Two

I decided to go back to school after a few failed attempts at getting life right. I felt like I didn't belong in the small town I lived in and knew there was more out in the world, more opportunities and achievements I couldn't wait to get my hands on. I needed a reset. I enrolled in an expedited graduate program to begin this new journey. Because I already had my Associate of Applied Science, I would earn my Bachelor of Applied Science in just one year—one academically intense year. Earning another degree in only a year sounded like the perfect fit because I had already lived my college years in small apartments with roommates and more late nights than I would have liked. I was over the idea of college as a whole, but my current degree wasn't going to get me the life I wanted. If I was going to go back, gain more student debt, and delay a full-time job again, it was going to be for only one year. I pride myself on my willingness to work hard and take anything on with a positive attitude, and I walked into this experience with that exact mentality. I toured the school and was very impressed by the staff members I met. They were poised, older ladies perfectly dressed in their tailored suits with freshly painted nails. They looked a little tired, which I should have taken as a subtle nod to my upcoming twelve months. They lectured me on the college's image and expectations for their students in regard to how they would dress, behave, and carry on the prestigious title after graduation. I fit their standards and agreed with them. It was a breath of fresh air hearing that I would be in an adult setting with professionals working toward a common goal.

I decided to participate in the live-in student program. In this program, local funeral homes agreed to hire students to work as minimally paid interns while living on the premises rent-free. Most funeral homes had housing connected to them because of the high demand and late nights the funeral directors endured. This program would allow me to apply what I learned each day in a hands-on setting. Not to mention I would be paid a small amount for my internship and receive free housing. In Chicago, rent was insanely high, so for me, it was an easy decision.

The kind ladies summed me up pretty quickly and, because of their first impression of me, offered me an opportunity to be their pioneer in this program. "You're so personable, Penelope. That's very important in this field." I was used to getting comments about being pretty or having good hair. While those comments were nice, it meant so much more to have a compliment from a stranger on anything other than my appearance. I'm certainly not one to hide from flattery, so when they informed me that it was a new contract with a funeral home that hadn't yet enrolled in the internship program and they felt I would make a great first impression for the college and open the door to a long relationship between the two. I nodded excitedly at the opportunity for an interview. It was a long drive to the funeral home, which was a red flag, but I chalked it up to city living and kept driving. Also, it was the only option left for internship housing, so the cons of a far drive versus high rent buffered the mileage. As I pulled into the parking lot and saw the sparkling water rippling onto shore, a shore only a foot below the edge of the parking lot, and an in-ground pool that overlooked the gleaming lake, my jaw dropped. I took a second after putting my car in park to inhale, exhale, and subtly put my fists on my hips in the effort to do a nonchalant power pose in my driver seat. "I can do this. It's going to be great," I whispered to myself before I unbuckled my seat belt and opened my car door. This location was beautiful, as was the funeral home. Freshly renovated and well kept, the building had older bones, I could tell from the outside, and it was located on a street surrounded by older homes, but I've always been a water baby, so the sparkling ripples called to me. I knew this was exactly where I was supposed to be.

The interview went very well, and the suite I would be living in was just that, sweet. It had floor-to-ceiling windows lining the west side of the wall, allowing for a huge, perfect view of every day's sunset. This was my new home, my new life, an accomplishment I was incredibly proud of. I had moved away from the home I had known up until this point and into foreign territory—territory with a brand-new Jacuzzi tub.

I was sitting in a chair at a table in the café of the college that would host the best year of my life. But right then, it felt very unknown, as did the strangers around me. We were all waiting to be called into our classroom to begin orientation and find out what exactly we had just signed up for. We strangers did what polite strangers do best, made small talk. I genuinely wanted to get to know the people around this table. We all appeared so different, yet all had the same career drive. I knew we had a lot in common. We were a wide range of ages, ethnicities, experiences, and stories, all trying to start a new path. From the late nights of studying, the new best friends I'd make, the local coffee spot I'd spend every after-school hour in, to the brutal exams, I was ready for it. There was, of course, the part I wasn't ready for. My red strings.

2

One Please

Everyone seemed pretty friendly, some were young, and some were heading into their second or third careers. It was an interesting collection of people, all so diverse. Some beat the stereotypes of what a funeral director looked like, and others fit it perfectly. A few made me feel like I was watching an episode of the *Addams Family*. I'm sure they were sizing me up too. I certainly didn't look like I could assist in lifting a casket or like I ever had dirt under my nails, but that wasn't true. I worked with a trainer to build muscle tone for this job specifically and I grew up riding ATVs through the mud just to see how messy I could get. I was more than a pretty face in an Anne Taylor suit and pumps. So, I shouldn't be making preconceived notions about their appearance either.

Around our small table, we discussed where we went to college previously, where we were from, and how we chose the career path we were all currently embarking on. I was attending an advanced, one-year course to become a funeral director. It was a well-known school, and graduates were almost guaranteed a quality job after graduation—assuming they could make it to graduation. I was taking in every second and trying to retain as many facts about the people at my table as I could so that when we crossed paths again, they'd know that I cared about the things they were saying and maybe we would even create a good friendship down the road.

Small talk was going well. We were laughing and getting along. Nora was talking about the puppy she had just gotten and how he loved to run around her family's funeral home. Apparently, it was a big thing coming up in the funeral service world to have a certified service dog greet your grieving guests with wet kisses and a wagging tail. It sounded like something I would certainly pay for. Terry was telling us about his daughter and how she had just moved to another state to further her college education; therefore, it was the perfect time for him to go back to school and fulfill his dream of being a comforting shoulder for people in need to lean on. I was surrounded by sweet, caring, high-quality people.

As I leaned back in my chair to get comfortable, my eyes naturally glanced up and clung to a tall guy who was standing by the cabinetry located near the entrance of the café. It housed the fridge, the microwave—stuff that in that moment I did not care about. While he was deep in conversation with a guy who looked to be about twice his age, he shifted a bit to his left to lean against the vending machine, and boy was I ready to pay for whichever letter and number combination would get me that fine human. Needless to say, my eyes stayed longer than expected, and my mind wandered, making whatever conversation was currently going on in front of me suddenly seem null and void. I was more focused on the smile that was so bright, beaming and utterly captivating that I inhaled deeply and wondered who the hell his dentist was and how I could get an appointment. I didn't know his name or where he was from. Was he nice? Was he interesting? Did he know how handsome he was? I had no idea who this person was, but I was drawn to him like a magnet. I wanted to know every last detail about him, and I was going to learn it the hard way.

3

Noted

The president of the college, Christina, greeted us and invited us to come into our future classroom. It was a unique setup. There were only two classrooms in the entire building. The library was bigger than both classrooms put together. I was used to having to book it across campus to make it to my next class on time, but here, we didn't change lots, buildings, or even rooms. All students in this orientation group would spend their year in one classroom, at the same desk, with the same people. The professors were the only ones who did any rotating. We picked seats that we all knew would be our seats for the majority of the year—until, of course, friend groups formed, and so-and-so had to sit by so-and-so because they were in a study group so they gathered in the back to share notes and so on. Without hesitation, I walked a little faster to be right behind my new crush and tried to play it cool as I pushed to get a seat near his. I slowly folded into the seat diagonally across from his to make it seem unintentional and placed my bag on the floor at my feet. I got out my notebook and a pen and started to take notes on start times, dress code, books required and recommended. Again, they began going over the expectations they had for us. I'd always been a notetaker, but that was just a nod to my poor memory. I was notorious for saying, "Oh, I'll remember that. No need to write it down" and then moments later kicking myself for the false confidence. Was I one of the only people taking notes? Of course I was. I would have hidden my geeky attentiveness, but if I was going to sit by this guy for an entire year, he'd have figured it out anyway. I figured I'd just get the bush out of the way and not even bother beating around it. I took notes, wore glasses, asked questions, hated technology, and overthought assignments—cue orientation day notetaking.

Minutes into orientation, we were prompted to do an icebreaker challenge and say a few facts about ourselves— our name, age if we wanted, where we were from, and our plans after graduation. Since I was in the first row of desks, it was my turn before I knew it. "Well, hello, I'm Penelope, but I prefer Nellie. I'm twenty-four … today actually. It's my birthday"—cue awkward hand gesture— "I'm from a very small town about four hours from here and would love to find a job in the city after graduation, maybe buy a fixer-upper in the suburbs and renovate it. It's always been on my bucket list, so I might as well try for it!" *Done. Heart, resume normal rate now please.* I would get so nervous speaking in front of people, especially for a first impression. There was just too much pressure to come off cool and collected. It was not like the questions were hard. I was guaranteed to sound like I knew what I was talking about. I was as good at answering questions about myself as anyone was, but I was also good at twisting my words around and stuttering mildly when I got nervous.

A few people later, it was smile guy's turn. "Hello, I'm Evan. I'm twenty-three and a third-generation funeral director at my family's funeral home, I plan to work there when I graduate."

Okay, I knew his name and age. Unfortunately, I had made a pact with myself that I would never ever date a guy younger than I was. I didn't feel he would be mature enough. High school and small-town community college students were all I had to go off of, and they hadn't done much in Evan's favor. *So sorry, guy with a cute smile, I'm not interested in babysitting.* In an academic sense, it was good—really good. Since I had a tendency to melt around cute boys and suffered from a staring problem, I was always reprimanded at parent-teacher conferences for being "too much of a social butterfly with the boys." It was almost like a rite of passage for each teacher I ever had to say that to my parents before I moved on to the next grade. Like I said before, boarding school. My mom never got the hint. So, on a brighter note, I could actually pay attention again and focus on being the best in my field. I know that sounds like a big dream, but I had a competitive side in the workplace. Plus, I had an inspiration board to live up to.

In addition to the verbal introductory icebreaker, the school set up a mixer at a bowling alley nearby for a few days later to get everyone mingling since we would be working very closely together over the next year. They encouraged us to study together and create flash cards—lots and lots of flash cards. They pushed the flash card subject so hard I began to wonder if they had stock in the local office supply store. Apparently, the four-year curriculum being smashed into one year wasn't enough of a frightening factor that they had to bring up the dropout rate. Forty-five percent of students didn't make it past the seventh month. That certainly put some fear into us all based on the suddenly erect posture and head turning I saw. The president alluded to our study schedule being our newest full-time job by advising us to study every single day for hours on end, as it was mandatory not to fall behind, which put a weird combination of intimidation and motivation in me. Perks of the expedited course, I supposed. I couldn't wait to put my pen to paper and get started writing notes and flash cards and soaking in every bit of information I could. This school was known for producing the best in the field, and I was determined to be one of the best.

4

Above Average

B*ring on the greased-up lanes.* It was the day of the mixer and time to kick off mingling with our course mates. In the past few days, I had gotten the hang of the new study schedule and had gotten to know the people in my immediate circle of desks, which included Evan and Taylor. Taylor was much more vocal than Evan was and would speak up to comment on eavesdropped conversations. He was kind of an open book, which is inevitable when your mouth is always open. I first found him annoying and brash, but similar to your first-ever cup of black coffee, he grew on me. He became one of my favorites quickly. I was very surprised to find out that Taylor grew up really close to where I was from. We even had mutual friends but never crossed paths until then. Talk about a small world. I was really hoping for a large world and to be in an area where there weren't any familiar faces, but I would take Taylor as the exception to that ideal. Heading into this year, I knew I wouldn't run into anyone from my small town because against my will, I knew everything about everyone from there, and no one but me was going into the funeral directing field. It wasn't exactly a common career path. However, I didn't take into consideration the towns surrounding mine. Hence, Taylor. He was friendly, funny, and a nice touch of home in the fast-paced city. His accent made me feel at home also; it was a subtle Southern accent with a twist of small-town grit. As the day went on and the early dismissal for the mixer got closer, I tossed some banter back to the guys. "I used to be in a bowling league, you know. You guys are going down."

Taylor ate it up and chuckled at my attempt to intimidate them, but Evan, who had not really spoken much until this point, shot a look up to me and blurted out, "What's your average?" with sheer excitement and intent. It was so out of character (as we knew his character to be in those few days) that we laughed, and he blushed. I smiled at him and told him that it was so long ago and I only did it for fun in high school that I didn't remember what my average was but assured him I was a moderately decent bowler and that he was, in fact, going down. That question never died as a joke between the three of us and probably never will. That was just one of the many useless details my brain holds on to. Between that and the Greek alphabet, among many other things, these facts were taking up storage room in my brain that could probably be better used to memorize the interior workings of the heart, but nope, I chose to retain one-liners and the alphabet to a country I'd never been to. Was it because that was the first thing he'd really ever said to me or because it was so genuine and surprising all at the same time that my crush started to build a little more? So I guess you could say he had me at "What's your average?" instead of *hello*.

Since they were the only two I really knew at that time, I hopped into Evan's truck with Taylor, and we headed off to the student mixer together. It was your average bowling alley and smelled like cheap pizza and used shoes. The sound of pins crashing drowned out the Top 100 list of the day's hits playing over the surround-sound speakers. It was a very windy day, so my hair swirled up, taking the shape of a tornado above my head as we walked in. I was uncomfortable to begin with because of the exhausting string of classes we had earlier that day mixed with the nerves of heading to a mixer full of strangers, leaving me with dry, tired eyes and small sweat marks on my shirt under my armpits that made me self-conscious. We no sooner hit the entryway than we were greeted with a twenty-four-by-thirty-six-inch board with teams pre-selected at random. Bowling teams were created by the administrators. I greeted the "welcome" poster with an eye roll. They broke us down into a mix of new students and existing students from the other classroom who would graduate six months before us, making room for the next group to begin in their classroom. I was a little disappointed to find out we couldn't select our own teams because, of course, I wanted my team to be composed of the people I knew and liked. Obviously, I was missing the point of a *mixer*. I'm happy to have been pushed outside of my comfort zone now, looking back at it, because our core friend group formed this day. No, we weren't all on the same bowling team; we were all spread out across the fourteen lanes we took up. We connected at the bar as we waited in line for our pitchers of beer—an unseen foreshadowing. While timing is everything, I'm convinced that even if we didn't become friends on this day, we would have on another day based on our similar schedules and daily routines. The sooner the better though because not only did I meet a group of strangers I would soon love dearly, but I learned that maybe this professional adult academy was a little less professional and a little more "I'll take a pitcher—no, two pitchers please." Who knew funeral directors were so much fun? I was too sheltered by my small-town life to correlate high stress and a mild flirtation with alcoholism, which would soon become a trend over the next year with these guys. My attention was being pulled in a million different directions. I was chatting with anyone in an arm's reach radius, yet I couldn't help but get a little jealous of the girl who got to be on Evan's team as he laughed with her about throwing her fourth gutter ball in a row—not in a way that made me feel that they were flirting or going to fall in love by any means but the type of jealousy that is purely insane to be honest. I was jealous that she was in his company and making him laugh and that I wasn't.

I refocused on being present in the moment, enjoying the people who were actually on my team, and getting to know them better. While they were funny and so friendly, I was more excited about my new group of friends, the group from the bar. We shot glances and waves and exchanged small talk back and forth as we lane hopped to trash talk each other's hand-eye coordination when the scores tallied up on the monitors. They were like familiar strangers at this point, but I was excited about knowing them. I had a feeling that they were going to be important parts of my life this year. Yes, I was the only girl in our forming friend group, but I liked it that way. I got to be one of the guys. I had a few rough times being bullied by other girls in junior high and high school, so I tended to gravitate toward the guys now out of emotional safety. It boded well for me in the long run. The president of the college noticed the group of us hit it off and suggested a photo to commemorate the day. I still have the picture of the five of us. It makes me smile every time I look at it. With the oversized bowling pin, a bowling ball in the background, and our baby faces smiling so genuinely, I understand the cliché phrase that a picture is worth a thousand words. We were fresh faced and unfamiliar. On that day, we didn't know what was in store for us over these next 365 days, but we were happy and ready for the ride.

I was feeling confident with my ability to retain the information I was learning in class. The professors recommended rewriting the notes we took in class once we got home as a way to retain the subject better. They went so far as to recommend we write them in blue ink; it helped with memory retention, I guess. This rewriting concept was a definite for me because my notes in the moment were sheer chicken scratch. It was by grace that I was even able to read them when I got home. If degrees were given out by merit, I would be an MD because my notes looked like a prescription or the information written out on the death certificates we were currently studying. I know it's not true, but I read an article that explained why people with bad handwriting were proven more intelligent than those with neat and clean handwriting. It was nonsense, but it helped me keep from internalizing any self-deprecating thoughts as I moved my paper side to side trying to figure out if that was an "a" or a "u" and wondering if those were two words smashed together or a hyphenated word. "It's okay, Nellie. You're just really, really smart."

I had my routine down and was comfortable in my new life just a fresh two weeks into it. My phone was constantly lighting up with alerts and running on low battery from the constant vibration of the group chat conversations and Snapchats I was getting from my forming friend group. I had a small bin full of those infamous flash cards and had filled up an entire notebook at that point. I passed my six exams and felt confident in the two research papers I wrote, one in psychology and the other in religion. I was surprised at the weight of the religion content covered, but the more I learned about psychology and ceremony, the more it made sense because we humans need assurance and comfort in a time of grief. We covered thirty-two religions over this year and were trained on how to conduct a funeral service in each.

My apartment was clean, and my laundry was caught up, which was the first time in my life I could say that and be able to take full credit for it. I was learning a lot on the job and impressing my bosses with my application of the subject matter that I had learned up to this point. I was answering questions that their resident intern stared blankly at. I was staying fit and felt very good about my physical appearance, my intelligence, and my social skills, not to mention I finally figured out how to get to the grocery store and home again without using my phone for directions. This confidence I was earning felt good. I was ready for a positive change in life—to be in control and ready to take on whatever was given to me with a smile and thorough execution.

5

High Hopes

We went on a date, Evan and I. A double date, actually. It was supposed to start out as Evan and I spending some time alone together. The original plan was to head downtown, have lunch together, see some touristy spots, and then make it back to his apartment in time to hang out with the other couple, Scott and Leah. She was so timid, and he was very bold but hilarious. Scott was in class with us, in our friend group too. Since the first day of classes, he was so eager to introduce us to his fiancé. Scott told us about a popular local bar he heard of and wanted to try out, so we planned to all go together and make it a double date.

I felt my stomach clench with excitement when Evan

texted me. There was something about seeing his name pop up on my phone that made everything else seem very unimportant.

Evan Ellis: Do you want to go downtown with me on Saturday before we hang out with Scott & Leah?

Me: Yeah, sure! What time?

Evan Ellis: Be at my place at 11. I've never been before, so I'll take your lead on how to get there.

Me: I'm very familiar. You're going to love it.

Evan Ellis: I hate cities and crowds, but I think you're right.

Was he saying that he knew he'd have fun because he was with me, or was I reading into that too much? I told myself he was just looking forward to not seeing a textbook out of the corner of his eye. Regardless of his reasoning, I was so excited for this day. I racked my brain for all of the places I would take him and looked up which trains we would take to which stop with an app I had. I knew what I was doing, but since I was "leading" him, I needed to *know* what I was doing.

Saturday morning came, and all of my newfound confidence and effort put into creating a fun day date went out the window. I got too nervous and never showed up to the first part of our date day. I got ready, looked cute, and had no other plans, but I couldn't bring myself to go. I texted him in the morning to tell him I was running late because of something that came up at work and would probably only make it to his apartment before we headed to dinner with Scott and Leah.

It was all a lie.

I was dressed, ready, and sitting on my couch scrolling through the guide, without even processing what my eyes were looking at on my oversized TV right before I sent that cancellation text. I had nothing else to do that morning, not even laundry, and I wasn't about to study any more— even with a gun to my head. I looked adorable in my new, torn-denim jeans, Converse, and band tee. My outfit was comfortable, but my insides were not. I was so anxious and could only think about everything that could go wrong.

Maybe I was intimidated by the date being an entire day. Which is understandable, I mean, come on, a whole day with a guy I only knew for a few weeks sounds crazy. Even though we had been friends for two weeks, he wasn't the most talkative in the group, so I didn't know much about him. Aside from his catchy "What's your average?" line, I had only gotten about five more sentences out of him directly. If I wanted a conversation with the guy, it was by text. He was more comfortable talking to me behind the screen. There wouldn't be screens between us in Chicago. I spiraled into a mini panic attack worrying about what I would do if there was an awkward silence or how I could come off as calm and cool while also being a tour guide and leading the way. Did he want me to teach him a little bit about downtown or would that be nerdy and lame? What would this guy even want to talk about for fifteen hours today? What I did know about him was that he didn't like cities and crowds, and since I have this people-pleasing tendency that won't allow me to force people into things they don't want to do, I wasn't ready to be that far out of my comfort zone. For all I knew, this wasn't even an official date. He never called it a date. He just asked me if I wanted to spend some time with him this weekend. I did want to spend time with him. Even though he was younger than me, he acted mature. He carried himself well and knew when to stay silent. He was kind and used his manners. My crush was growing back, so of course I wanted to go and was upset with myself that I just couldn't.

His volunteering to go to a very crowded, people-filled downtown to hang out with me is what made me think he was interested in me as well. You don't volunteer to do something you hate unless it's with someone you like. I do really wish I would have just gone now that I think back to it, but although I had the confidence, I didn't have the courage that I have now.

When I finally got to Evan's apartment, Scott and Leah were less than five minutes away, so alone time for us had really dissolved. The four of us ended up just hanging out in his living room for a little bit and smoking. Yes, I know, I'm not courageous enough to spend a day with a crush but doing drugs with moderate strangers, this I've got in the bag. The new round of paranoia that kicked in wasn't about doing drugs in a foreign apartment with two guys twice my size and a girl I had just met; it was needing to pee. An odd concern but the high had kicked in, and the gallons of water I had chugged had taken their toll. I'd been pretty quiet because of shyness and uncertainty about what I planned to say in my head. Would it make me sound like I was high? I hate when people go all Bob Marley off of two hits, so I was cautious not to be that person. Scott even commented on my silence, asking me if I was okay. *Great*, I thought, *to get up now would only make me seem like I'm getting up to leave the room*, as if I were offended by the actually offensive, yet comical, video they were watching on Scott's phone. But I couldn't ask where the bathroom was as a buffer when I got up to leave because it was a tiny apartment; everyone knew where the bathroom was. I was out of options. I had been quiet for so long that if I spoke now, my high, paranoid self feared that it would be awkward. So I just held it, crossing my legs and banning any more water, hoping that eventually I would be able to gain the guts to just get up and pee like an adult. But oh no, that was not the end of it. My later growing concern was that his bathroom was right by the living room so they would definitely hear me peeing, and since I had held it for so long, it was sure to be one of the world's longest pees. I was doomed. Another twenty minutes passed, and at this point, I knew it was get up or pee on his couch. Word to my past self: Maybe don't smoke with people you hardly know, want to impress, and possibly want to date if you're socially awkward when you're high. Repeat.

We ordered an Uber to take us to the best local restaurant, and I don't mean best as in high quality but best as in food that made you drool. It wasn't fancy. It even had a drive-through, one that was notorious for having a line so long that it wrapped around the building at any time of the day. It also had cake shakes, juicy beef sandwiches, and cheese fries from your wildest cheese fry dreams. As my paranoid high wore off, my hunger broke through, and I ate a big plate of grease, making myself uncomfortably full without remorse. We then did what everyone dreams of doing when you've overeaten and are six-months-pregnant kind of bloated; we headed over to the bar for drinks and dancing. It was a really cool country-themed bar with a giant guitar cut out on the ceiling and live country music. It's closed down now. They've turned it into a restaurant. I gasped with heartache when I found out about it closing down. I'd be lying if I said I wished the restaurant well. I did nothing short of whine about the influx of restaurants and food greed in America. Not my shining moment, but I loved that bar. It was my kind of place. I was really hoping to revisit it sometime to reminisce on the fun we had under those color-changing lights. Now all of those memories are stuck in the past, in our memories and camera rolls only.

I was so happy to be with this new group of friends and in this great bar that flirted with my country roots. As I looked up and down, soaking in the repeating theme and unique architecture of the space, Scott made his way to the very crowded bar before any of us could, to get everyone's first round. In an effort to be agreeable and easy, Evan and I went with the same beer Scott had ordered for himself.

A few sips later, Evan looked at me and said, "I have to switch to liquor. This is too heavy, and I'm beyond full from dinner." He was reading my mind word for word.

"I'm with you; my stomach is too full for beer. I'm going to explode."

Every girl says that on a first date, right?

It was in that moment he set his beer down, placed his hand on my lower back, smiled, and grabbed my beer from my hands to place on the bar next to his. "Can we get two …" He paused and looked at me for approval. "Vodka, water, and limes?"

I nodded agreeably with a smirk of appreciation at his assertiveness. As the bartender started making our drinks in her adorable Daisy Duke getup, Evan told me that the drink coming my way was his go-to for liquor and that it was ranked the healthiest of the cocktails and had the fewest calories per the article he had read a few months ago. Why this guy even monitored calories was beyond me, but I appreciated his gesture and that damn smile.

A few vodka, water, limes, and dances later, Leah leaned over to me and told me that Evan had been staring at me all night and that she loved the way he looked at me—so intentionally. After my cheeks got nice and blushed, I told her how cute I thought he was and a little bit about our conversations we had while she and Scott were off dancing together. She told me that I should go for it if I was interested. Now I'm not the type of girl to "go for it," but I was open to *him* going for it. We had drink after drink and dance after dance. Before we knew it, the band started packing up and the lights turned on, revealing the many spilled-drink puddles all over the dance floor and the sweaty hair we were all donning. As we walked to the door to leave, Evan put his hand behind him as an invitation for me to grab it. We walked into the chilly night air hand in hand and waited for our ride home to arrive. I started wiggling my knees back and forth a bit in an effort to keep warm. Seconds later, Evan wrapped his arms around me to keep me warm in a big bear hug fashion. I could feel him looking down at me, so I looked up at him knowing what was coming next. Right there under the streetlight and dark sky, he kissed me. The first kiss was gentle and soft, and then a second and third followed with a little more passion. I pulled away only to release the smile I'd been holding back, but I didn't want the kissing to end. This night had been incredible. I was kissing cute smile guy, and it was under the most beautiful night sky. I promised myself I would never forget this moment. Like in the Etta James song, a spell was cast.

We slept together that night. There was no making him wait or earning trust before the next step. I wanted him.

In fact, I wanted him in the parking lot as we shared our first kiss, so I give myself kudos for waiting until we made it back to his apartment. It was just drunk sex. There's no romanticizing it. I hardly remember the details of it to be honest, not because I wasn't writing it down in my notebook but because vodka has a way of allowing us to forget the drunken things we do. Sometimes it's for the best. But in this case, I wished it hadn't. I wanted to remember every detail about the first time I took that step with him. But the next thing I remember, I was waking up on the soft, smooth skin of his chest. I took a moment to replay the night in my head as his heartbeat played in my left ear. My head was pressed up against the nook between his shoulder and ribcage. He was tall and thin, yet surprisingly comfortable to lie on. I soaked up the feeling of the perfect puzzle-like fit our bodies made and the few details of his room that I could see without moving my head. His closet was long and shallow. I could see everything in it because it didn't have doors. It looked like there used to be a sliding accordion door because there was a track running along the top of it. It was an older apartment. Wallpaper trim lined the top of his walls. I saw his cotton tees hanging in a disheveled manner but separated from his dress shirts and suits. The entire left side was filled from floor to ceiling with paper towel and toilet paper, which he obviously bought in bulk. I wondered if he also bought his condoms in bulk or if our first date hook-up was just as out of character for him as it was for me. It felt less romantic after that thought, and I got up to head home. He didn't wake up to my movement, he only moved the arm I had been laying on. He was out cold with only the assumed four hours of sleep he got up until that point. I was an early riser whether I was out late the night before or not. I didn't want to wake him up. I wanted to sneak out and remain somewhat aloof, saving some dignity after giving him the entire farm on our first date. My long drive home was spent in disbelief of the night I had just had. He already had me wrapped around his finger, and needless to say, I was antsy to see him again. I wanted to start this "something new" with this "something handsome."

6

Just A Game

I felt pretty self-conscious about my "game." I had heard in the past that I either tried too hard or seemed disinterested, so I tried to find the middle ground, especially in this intended "growing year," and once this handsome hunk had me interested, I didn't want to blow it. Staying low key, letting him text me first, and not using too many words or showing too much excitement in my replies were just some of my tactics during this weekend apart. I even went as far as making sure that my hair wash cycle lined up perfectly to when I'd see him again so that just in case he hugged me, I would be perfectly groomed and smell like a soft brush of tea-tree oil because guys notice those things, right? Days had gone by, but we kept in touch, texting back and forth with updates on our days and some subtle flirting. He had barrels of charisma, and it showed through in his texts. He played the anticipation game of waiting a few minutes to text me back, which drove me nuts, but his replies were always thought out and full sentences, so it came off as he was really thinking about what to say instead of watching the clock before sending me "cool" or "ok." When the two-minute mark hit. Maybe he was googling how to flirtatiously text a girl and copying the results into his texts because he was excelling. He asked me questions about myself and answered the questions I asked him without hesitation to open up, or so it seemed at least. I was working for the funeral home I lived above, as we were getting to know each other via text. There wasn't much on my list of responsibilities as a student worker. I didn't have a license to legally do any of the important things and was not experienced enough to be trusted with more than answering the phones, filing paperwork, and greeting the guests as they arrived. I was not one to sit around and twiddle my thumbs, so on the days like this particular day, when my only duty was to answer the phone if it rang, I found myself creating work for myself to stay busy. I would dust light fixtures or wipe down the desks, even vacuum the tightest corners of the office with the detailing attachments. Because of my extra work, I was seen with high regard by my bosses and coworkers, which was a nice welcome into the team. They liked walking into a clean office with an organized desk in the morning. Once my self-created additional list of chores was complete, I felt more comfortable sitting in my office chair waiting for the phone to ring and texting Evan in my downtime, with no guilt lingering over my head. He replied quickly and kept my attention by making me laugh out loud occasionally. I was thankful I was in the office alone because when he asked me where I wanted to go on my honeymoon, I gasped just before my jaw hit the floor. I couldn't believe my eyes. I'd never known a guy to bring up anything regarding marriage or post-marriage, especially this early on in the relationship, but I didn't hate it. I didn't jump to any conclusions or think he assumed he might possibly be invited to such a vacation until he replied with a photo of Santorini and a caption agreeing how beautiful Greece would be as a honeymoon destination. What's an appropriate response to something like that? "Yes, I'll marry you." "I love you too." "I'm packing my bags." I took the less obvious route of "I could use a gorgeous vacation like that right about now. Sun, sand, and good food!" I continued to receive spontaneous pictures of the coast of Greece days and weeks following this conversation. He paid attention to me saying that I loved the contrast of the white buildings and the bright-blue water because, as proof, every photo had white buildings and bright-blue water. We had really hit our relationship hard that first night, and while it turned out very well, from the clips I remember at least, we both knew we needed to lay some sort of a foundation if it was going to be anything more than a one-night stand. We had slowed down now and took it step by step. It was surreal getting to know him. He had such a spell on me from the beginning that I put him on a pedestal and clung to every word he said. I wanted to know everything about him. We balanced our friendship with our growing romance while keeping it to ourselves. I was the only girl in the group of us, so I didn't want to bring the relationship drama into the group. We kept our romantic side a secret, which only made it more exciting—shooting glances and winks and hand grabs as we passed each other in the halls at school. It was going very well. He made me feel beautiful and interesting. As he learned more about me, he continued to ask more and more.

About two weeks after we began building up our relationship and learning more about each other, he invited me to a professional hockey game—but not just any professional hockey game and not just your average seats. He had sixth-row seat tickets right behind the goal for a Blackhawks game. They were my favorite of any team or sport. They had really started to peak around this time and were on a winning streak. They even claimed the Stanley Cup, which is equivalent to winning the Super Bowl. *How did he get these tickets? Is this guy real?* I was living what was shaping up to be my favorite year of my life, and I was only a month into it. Staring at dream tickets in the hands of my dream guy—pinch me. I had been a Blackhawks fan for years, and he knew it. He probably figured it out after I wore a jersey once or twice to class to support my boys on game day or from the multiple Snapchats I sent him disclosing my love as I watched their games. I remember getting the text with a picture of four tickets in his lap like it was yesterday. I squealed and checked the picture maybe twenty times in disbelief, looking for a prank somewhere in the picture and making sure they weren't fake tickets before I replied with "One of those is mine, right? Please tell me I can go with you!" I was beside myself. I had been to games in the past but never even close to the sixth row.

"Of course one is for you. I want you to teach me about these guys."

Who is this guy? And how did I get so lucky? Something's going to break soon, right? No one is supposed to be this happy. I was thankful this was all over the phone and not in person, because one of his winks or a smile in this moment would have quite literally liquefied me.

Since he had four tickets, he invited Scott and Taylor to go also. I happily drove the four of us to the game. It was the least I could do since I was getting my dream game tickets for free, plus all the guys had trucks and I had a compact car that could fit in any tiny parking space we found downtown. He wouldn't let any of us pay him back for the tickets. It was genuinely a kind gesture. He just wanted to treat us to a fun night out. He succeeded.

To kick off the long, forever-running strand of being the butt of the guys' jokes, they had plenty to say about my driving in the downtown traffic and shrieked about feeling unsafe multiple times. I didn't care. I was on cloud nine. I filled the guys in on the game of hockey and the world of "Hawkey." I was a kid in Santa's workshop—this was where the magic happened. I wanted to teach them what to chant and when as well as the terminology of hockey. I explained what a hat trick was, the penalty format, and how they structured overtime. None of the guys were into hockey. Evan got us the tickets as a fun thing for us to do together in the city, not because he was a fan of the sport. They all smiled at my innocent excitement and rolled their eyes at my comments about the players during warm-up stretches. If you haven't watched hockey players do warm-up stretches, especially the goalie, look it up. You're welcome in advance. I kept shifting my eyes over to Evan to make sure he was enjoying himself. In the middle of the game, he put his arm around me and glanced over at me with a smirk and a wink. It was kind of uncomfortable because of how the chairs were so I leaned my head on his shoulder for only a second before he pulled away. I was immediately embarrassed. My first reaction was to assume I did something wrong. He obviously pulled away because I took it one step too far. I shouldn't have put my head on his shoulder. I wanted to readjust because I was uncomfortable, and I wanted to make some sort of gesture so he knew I liked that his arm was around me at the same time. He was different for the rest of the night too, quieter and more unattached. This was the first time I noticed him pulling back or shutting me out, so I didn't know where it came from or why he would pull away after bringing me through this unforgettable night. Just when I thought nothing could bring me down from my cloud, I spent the next few hours wondering what had set him off.

The rest of the night was still incredible—just a group of friends having a good time in the city. The next day, I texted Evan to thank him for the tenth time for the tickets and to let him know that I had had a wonderful night and was so appreciative. I didn't hear back from him for hours, and then my phone lit up with a text saying, "You bet. Glad you had fun." I tried to carry on the conversation but got stopped by him telling me that he needed to clarify he wasn't interested in dating anyone this year. "I want to focus on just having a good time and making memories with friends."

I felt my stomach flip because it didn't make sense to me. Why the turn and the change? So I asked him. "Where is this coming from?"

"It's always been my priority. I just thought I should make it clear."

Good thing he made it clear because it was apparently quite foggy beforehand.

"I've done many things with you that I haven't done with any other friend before, so the clarification was pretty mandatory."

I was pissed and sad and couldn't decipher which emotion was more prevalent. I wanted to do to the cliché belly-flop onto my bed and sob, but the balance of the pissed emotion prevented any pity party as did my low-grade, non-spring-loaded mattress. I stopped replying to him. I didn't know what else to say. I was so caught off guard that he could flip from saying all the right things and showing such interest to then pulling away a little bit and then even more, claiming that he wanted no form of romantic relationship with anyone. I didn't believe him. At the moment, I was certain there was someone else he was interested in. I stewed over it for a few hours with some comfort food until I remembered that I was better than this and that I could shake him off and focus on having fun also.

There was a very handsome guy in the class graduating before ours. We had met at the bowling mixer. He came on strong, so I shut him down, but his interest was still annoyingly apparent. He had been texting me periodically since the mixer. I didn't reply to any of his messages except the first one, in an effort to be polite. He got my number from another classmate and texted me, asking if we could just hang out. "I can tell you aren't interested in going on a date, but how about coming to hang out with me and some people? Just as friends. I think you're cool."

Thank you for the compliment, Mr. GQ, but I'm not cool—especially not as "cool" as all of your friends and exes look on your Facebook page. They all looked like they came from family money and would turn their nose at any outfit that didn't contain at least one item from a designer whose name was hard to pronounce. However, he did say that he was interested in me despite my sweater being from Target, so what the heck?

"Okay, let's hang out," I replied.

He was beyond gorgeous and said he was okay with being friends, and Evan "released" me, so I didn't see any reason to say no. Also, there was a small possibility of making Evan jealous, and I was there for it.

Days passed since I first hung out with Josh and his friends. They were actually a really entertaining group of people. They were friendly and cracked a lot of jokes while I was over there, so the laughter was a nice icebreaker. Much to my surprise, Josh didn't try anything on me—no longing looks into my eyes, no attempt to grab my hand. He was respectful of my desire to be just friends. He even opened the door to his brand-new, custom-designed, blacked-out Jeep every time I got in or out of it. This guy was great. We could talk for hours without any dead air. We talked about our families, goals, and likes and dislikes. He gave me a lot of tips and tricks about the course we were taking in school because he was six months further in than I was and wanted to save me any additional work just to learn something the hard way.

One of my favorite memories of hanging out with him was in the burst of summer. The days of uncertain weather were behind us, and it was just warm air now. Car windows were down, and apartment windows stayed open all day. I was told that it was the simple moments in a relationship that matter the most, being able to do nothing with someone and enjoy yourself. Granted, we were only friends, but I got a rush of joy and comfort when we were sitting on his couch eating our takeout and watching our rival baseball teams play against each other while the sun flirted with the idea of setting. I heard a car being locked by its fob—that series of beeps you hear that usually mean nothing but to assure the owner of the vehicle that he or she had succeeded in locking the door with just the push of a button. I know that sounds odd. I've heard that noise so many times all year, but for some reason, in that moment, it was euphoric. Still to this day, when I hear that noise in the summer, it soothes me.

We had been hanging out repeatedly for a few weeks as friends, almost every other day it seemed, and despite his drop-dead gorgeous looks and impeccable fashion sense, I wasn't attracted to him until I realized the ease and joy he brought me. I'm not the girl to make the first move, but I leaned toward him and grabbed the back of his neck while kissing him on the cheek. He turned his body and put his hand on my lower side in an effort to continue to a proper kiss. I didn't want to push it too far though, so I just smiled at him, chuckled, and eased out of his grip. The grin on his face was so proud that I started laughing and continued back to my oversized slice of pizza.

"I don't usually get kissed by my friends over dinner," he said while holding back a smile.

"You didn't seem to hate it," I said as I returned my grinning glance back to the TV in an effort to avoid him bringing up any conversation that would suggest us being more than friends yet.

He was very old-fashioned and liked to do things in the proper order to his beliefs, so after kissing, the next step was to become boyfriend and girlfriend. I was still mentally caught up with the idea of Evan and me possibly working out, so I wasn't ready for anything structured with anyone else. Josh and I continued to hang out with each other any moment that I wasn't studying or hanging out with my original friend group consisting of Taylor, Scott, and Evan—yes, Evan. Even though he didn't want a relationship, we still had an awesome friend group that nobody would voluntarily give up, so we all continued to hang out and study together.

It was a great dynamic until Scott came to my apartment a few minutes before the other guys did to get the "dirt" on me hanging out with Josh. "So, who's this dreamboat you've been hanging out with recently? I heard you guys are maybe dating. Is that true?"

It was a small trade school, so word spread like it does in a small town. Luckily, growing up in a small town buffered me for when all of my personal information continued to be shared among my peers.

"Are you not going to date Evan?" he continued prying.

Evan and I had been very good about keeping our dating life private from our friends, or so we thought.

"Evan called it quits a few weeks ago. He said he wants to continue to be friends but nothing more," I clarified.

"It's hard to believe considering I can still cut the tension between you two with my pinky finger."

"Well, believe it. Josh and I are just hanging out right now, and we haven't talked about dating yet. Who made you think we might be dating? I don't want that getting around. Especially to Evan."

Taylor's infamous laughter cut me off as he and Evan came up the stairs together. You could hear Taylor's laughter from miles away and instantly recognize it. It was a laughter that was contagious at first because if anything, you were laughing at his laugh. It then became a little annoying until it finally settled as normal. We went right on into our night of studying, drinks, laughing, and relaxing afterwards to say "cheers" to a job well done once we all felt ready for the upcoming tests we had the next day. My phone went off as we were all in my living room watching the tail end of a movie to cap off our night.

Evan xo: Josh?

Me: What about him??

Evan xo (I should have changed his contact name but never got around to it): Stay the night tonight.

Me: ?

I looked up at him hoping for some sort of clarification, but he was locked on the TV and not moving his eyes until he felt the quiet vibration of my reply. Then, he looked down at me with just a smirk and returned his gaze to the TV. Even if I wanted to stay, I couldn't. I was on call to answer the phones at the funeral home I lived in. I had to be there to cater to the incoming calls because at that hour of the night, calls were imperative. This meant that someone had passed away and the callers needed to inform us so we could begin preparing to go get their loved one and bring them into our care. This is a common practice in the funeral home. Phone management is vital. Evan, being in the business, understood that very well. Without any hesitation or shifted guilt, he didn't have to tell me that he understood. I knew he did. He simply said, "Walk me down at least." My mind immediately focused on why he didn't ask to stay at my place with me. And where did this immediate urge to have me stay over come from? Could he possibly be jealous of Josh? This could really work out in my favor.

Taylor and Scott headed out, and Evan made an excuse to be the last to leave. As I walked him down to the door, he turned around, wrapped me in his arms, pushed me up against the glass door, and kissed me like he'd been waiting weeks to do it. His fingers went from running through my hair, down my torso, and onto the waistline of my sweatpants without his lips ever skipping a beat. I could feel my blood warming up in my body as it rushed through me. My heart started to vibrate in my chest. I wanted to rip his shirt off with my bare hands but instead pulled my head back into the one inch of space it had before it hit the door.

"Hold on. Where is this coming from?" I asked.

"You can't act like you don't love it," he replied.

"I didn't say I didn't love it. But I think you're up to something, and I'm not sure I like the game behind it, so I'm just going to say good night and I'll see you tomorrow." I smiled sweetly at the end of that brash statement to make sure it came off flirty and not bitchy.

He kissed my forehead before heading out of the door to my right. To be honest, I didn't make him stop because of Josh. I completely forgot Josh existed in that moment. I made him stop because I didn't want him to think he could walk all over me and decide when we would be together and when we wouldn't. I wanted to take a stand and show him that I had a say in us as well. Thirty seconds later, I regretted making him stop. As I climbed the stairs to go back up to my apartment, I was kicking myself for pushing him out the door.

The next morning, we were back into our same routine. You would never know if we liked each other or were just acquaintances and especially not that we had made out the night before. He was all about subtleties, which made reading him harder because it assisted in the mind game of *Is this really something, or is he just flirting?* He was so private and secretive that no one else ever saw his soft side in public.

He would make comments or hints about things we talked about when it was just us, so I knew he meant more though no one else picked up on it.

I had passed my midterm test that week and texted Josh to brag since he claimed it was too hard to pass. He replied with an invitation to join his study group out for a celebratory lunch at my favorite restaurant. It was an instant yes, but it would take a bit longer to drive and eat there than we were allotted for lunch. We had to leave that second if we wanted to make it back in time for our afternoon classes. That would mean skipping out on the last half of this class, but since it was intro to our next topic, I felt I could get away with it. I sat at the opposite end of the door and right in front of Evan. Also, the back wall of the classroom was made of windows overlooking the parking lot, so when I packed my bag, got up, and walked across the classroom and right into Josh's car, nosey Evan saw every step. So did about fifteen other people in the class. That only put confirmation on the rumor that Josh and I had been hanging out. They all assumed it was in a dating manner, which was fine. Their perception was their reality, and I was in no position to waste time correcting them just to lose the battle. Evan gave me an ice-cold shoulder when I returned. He even bailed on our plans to hang out that night, so it was just me, Scott, and Taylor who went out to a movie and dinner together. We still had a great time, but I missed having him there. We sent him a picture of the three of us saying we wished he was there with us. I meant it more than the other two did. Turns out he just stayed in, watching TV at home. He was clearly just avoiding me. He didn't ask me for clarification or details about where I went. He went right to putting up his wall and pushing me out—a trait that I would love to change.

7

The Way We Do

The guys played in a golf outing the school puts on every year. I've never swung a golf club in my life, so I sat that one out. Since it was school-wide, my group of friends and Josh's group of friends merged together and really hit it off. It was convenient to have my two friend groups become one so that we could hang out together and I wouldn't miss out on one group for the other. It didn't go as smoothly as I thought because Evan and Josh weren't too fond of each other. Josh had every reason to dislike Evan, that made sense to me. Josh had feelings for me, and I was still swooning over Evan. However, I made it clear to Evan that Josh and I were just friends but no matter what was said, he heard what he wanted to. Once Evan believed something to be true, no one could ever convince him otherwise.

Sammy, one of Josh's friends, suggested throwing a small party that Thursday, and since Evan's place was the go-to spot for parties, he hosted. I was bummed when I heard about it because Josh had a hockey league game that I had planned to go to. I was excited to go watch him because it was a tournament game. I had gone to about six others, so I was invested in the team and wanted to see them take the tournament. I could get very competitive with sports, especially hockey. I was riddled with FOMO and couldn't help but give my phone the majority of my attention at work that day. The group text was going crazy with plans for the night, and it was sounding really fun. I played the loyalty card and couldn't bring myself to ditch plans with Josh.

Apparently, the drinking kicked in early, and as I learned later, a bet started over whether Evan could convince me to cancel my plans with Josh and come hang out with him instead. Turns out, Evan wasn't as mature as I originally thought. I hadn't told Evan I was hanging out with Josh that night instead of the party because I didn't want to stir the pot, but someone did it for me. I had a few more hours of work when I got a call from Evan. He was laying the flirtation on hard and saying that everyone at the party wished I was there and that he did too. He told me how much he missed me and that he wanted to talk to me that night, just us two. In my naive excitement, I agreed to come over and told him I'd be there in a few hours. I then texted Josh to let him know not to expect me at his game and that I wasn't going to make it after all but wished him the best of luck. Even though Josh was incredibly charming and mature, he didn't have the pull on me that Evan did. No one compared. I gave in to Evan almost every time he pulled for me. Not to mention, he had been dropping a lot of romantic cues my way in the week leading up to that day. I was ready for him to say that he was wrong about not wanting to date and that he was ready to start over and try dating again.

When I got to his apartment, the room roared with "Evaaaaan! Yesss!"

I didn't expect it, so I just laughed as my friends drunkenly greeted me. I sat down on Evan's lap as a response to his double hand tap on his thigh.

"What's the cheering about?" I asked as I took one of the last sips left of his beer.

"I told them I could get you to ditch your plans with Josh and come hang out with me. Because you're wrapped around my finger, of course," he spewed with confidence and charm.

"Your ego is showing," I said as I got up to get a drink.

He grabbed me by my hips, pulled me down, and asked where I was going.

"To get a drink. Want one?"

"Oooh yes, bartender." He winked.

I kind of felt shitty for ditching Josh, but I reassured myself that I wasn't bad to do so because he was having a blast at his game, probably winning, and it was not like we were dating anyway. *He will understand.* One of his friends at the party reassured me that he in fact would not understand and that he would care because he really liked me and wanted to date me all the while being intimidated by Evan because of rumors that had gone around the school about us. We hadn't been as secretive as we'd thought, and apparently this wasn't a graduate college; it was a chatty coffeehouse.

I talked with Josh the next morning to see how his game

had gone and to see if they had won. He told me he was okay with me skipping his game until he found out that I had stayed over at Evan's that night. That was crossing the line in his flirtatious friend handbook, which honestly, I understood. It made sense. He had feelings for me, and I was pushing him back. Because he didn't believe in friends with benefits or sleeping together before you were officially a couple, he was floored and upset that I had *slept with Evan*. I tried to correct him and tell him that I only literally slept, eyes closed and dreaming, with Evan, which was true. My drive home was so long, and I wanted to just have some drinks and relax with the group instead of worrying about my intake, monitoring it, and driving an hour home, just to turn around and drive an hour back in the morning. He lived right next to the school, so close that I could walk, so I stayed there often for that very reason—well, that reason and a few obvious others. We consistently tried to be sneaky so as not to cause any friction in the friend group. This time, word had definitely gotten around though. I blamed it solely on Evan because he grabbed me by my arm in front of everyone while I was in the living room and flirtatiously walked backward while pulling me to his room, which meant passing everyone in his apartment. The cherry on the cupcake was that he locked the door right after shutting it which in an older apartment, makes an obvious clicking noise. He kissed me just once. It was a long, soft kiss. His lips were so full and soft, like I remembered. This time, they smelled specifically like whiskey as he whispered in my ear that he wanted to lie with me and wrap himself around me "the way we do." He loved when I would lay my head on his chest and trace his ribs with each of my fingers slowly before falling asleep in his arms. In my experience, guys would pull away after I fell asleep because sleeping while wrapped up in someone else isn't always comfortable and can get too warm, but he did the opposite. If I went to turn away, he would turn to follow me, wrapping his arms around me and pulling me in tightly. It woke me up slightly each time but never so much that I couldn't fall right back to sleep with his arms around me and a grin on my face. Even as he was sleeping, he was so aware of where I was and wanted to be right there with me. We were magnetic.

8

S.O.S.

"I'm not ready to be in a long-term relationship. I want to be young and dumb. I want to drink too much, make stupid mistakes, and just have fun with new friends. I don't want to worry about my responsibilities or future right now" was followed up with "I want to be with you but not right now."

These words replayed in my head on repeat. The response I got when he told me he didn't want to date anyone during this year of school was very much in conflict with his actions. I wanted clarification on how he felt because I was getting mixed signals. He was physically and mentally pulling me in just to push me back out at his convenience. His pulling me in felt so genuine though. That was what made the pushing me back out so heart crushing. I could recognize the fuckboy, the player, the game, but this wasn't that. It was like he was really falling for me but had enough self-control to push me away, just not enough to move slowly with us. As much as I loved the ride and wanted so badly to be able to tell my head to be silent and just enjoy every second of every moment that I got with him, I couldn't help but second-guess what he was saying or wondering where it was going to go next. Did he only want to claim his territory, knowing that he could? A surely won fight? Did he want to make sure I was still on his reel so that he could bring me in and cast me out as he wanted?

What got me the most worked up was when I would text him and he wouldn't answer me for hours or even all day. *I know you see your phone. I know you saw my text.* It would wreck my mood for the majority of the day. I couldn't wrap my head around why he wouldn't reply. He went from attentive texting as his main form of communication to now, a whole different person. I would overthink my wording or timing or if he was trying to send me a subliminal message. Sometimes, I caved and sent a follow-up text to nudge a response, and when I still wouldn't get one, I felt like a mental patient. I started hating myself for caring so much. I couldn't tell whom I hated more though—him for doing this to me, or me for caring. The torturous part was when my phone would go off, and I'd get a rush of relief and excitement only to find out that it was a social media notification, an email or anything but his stupid response. Then, as time passed, I would get a phone call from him instead of a text back. Apologizing for thinking that he responded to me but that he just didn't hit send. I played into it but never really believed him.

Since Josh was mad at me for staying over at Evan's, he ignored me for a few days, which was what Evan wanted, it gave us more time to get close again. We kept up our secret relationship, growing in the dark, and loved every second of time together. We learned more about each other's family and upbringing. He taught me the cute sayings his family came up with as a way to say, "I love you," in a custom way. It was fitting for him to avoid using the L word while still showing the emotions it stood for. I was determined to heal him from his past heartbreaks that he told me all about. I tried to convince him that if he would just trust me and let me in, I wouldn't hurt him. I could tell he either wasn't truly listening to me or just didn't believe me by the blank look on his face and his efforts to change the topic.

He wasn't a fan of talking about his feelings and didn't like talking about the past very often. His job was circled around people's feelings and their needs. So even though he played dumb to emotion, he felt it and he knew how to handle it. He was trained to cater to others. As a funeral director, your life isn't really your own. You are on call either every day or most days, depending on the size of the staff. Being on call means that your phone could ring at any time of the day, whether 3:00 a.m. or 11:00 p.m., and you have to get dressed and go to work. Death doesn't care if you're on a date or finally getting to sit down after a long day of work. One could advise that you just don't schedule parties or events on the days that you're on call, but if you're a small, family-owned funeral home, that isn't a possibility. If you never scheduled things when you were on call, you would never schedule things. Therefore, you wouldn't have much of a personal life. What's worse is sitting at home all alone just waiting for your phone to ring any minute, and then it doesn't, and you waste a night sitting at home all day while your family or friends go out to dinner and a movie. Christmas morning could be taken from you, so could your birthday or the big game you've been waiting all day to watch. So, when he vented to me about his frustrations on this, I made sure to listen because he did the same for me. He said it was one of the reasons he really wanted to marry someone in the funeral directing field—someone who *got* it. He had been on dates in the past and had to cancel plans last minute because of a call coming in while he was working at his family's funeral home, and like clockwork, the girl got mad at him or tired of the disappointment over time and ended up breaking up with him because of it. I was a girl who understood. I wouldn't think twice when he needed to get up, answer a call, and then head out to go meet with the family. I would understand because I would be in his same predicament many times, and he would have to return the understanding. It was the nature of the job. It was easier on couples who were both funeral directors, or who at least had a similar on-call status. It felt good to talk to him about the future, our goals, and expectations. It was comforting to know he thought about us in the same way I did when it came to the future. I joked with him that I wanted *'til death do us part* written on our wedding invitations. I got a chuckle and smirk out of him, which wasn't a "no."

- - -

It felt like we were building our relationship and growing closer since we were spending so much time together. We had talked about everything under the sun, but something still wasn't right. Physically, we were on point and not just when it came to sex. Our bodies were in sync. Our pre-existing magnetism was stronger than before but also in a calmer, less urgent manner. It was more soothing now when he would wrap me up in his arms and give me big hugs from behind with a soft kiss on my cheek. But when we were in public, he was still a whole different person. I know that we tried to keep our relationship a secret but damn. He did it so well that I started to wonder if I had dreamed up all of the loving parts of him until eight hours later when he turned it on all over again. When I asked him about his night-and-day personality shifts, he replied with a stern response that we weren't dating.

"We're only friends," he would say.

This guy had me so confused. We had talked about us in the future together, the way you would with a boyfriend or girlfriend. I got that he wasn't one for PDA, so when we hung out with our friends or when we were out to dinner, a movie, the bars, running errands, or anywhere other than in either of our apartments alone, I got a limited display of affection. I wasn't confused about that part. For the most part, I was okay with it because to an extent, I was on the same page. There's nothing worse than trying to eat your dinner while the strangers next to you are inspecting each other's tonsils, but I wasn't as good at making it as black and white as he could. That was the part I wasn't on the same page with. I didn't want to be in a relationship that was so strictly black and white, I needed some gray. How could he tell me we're only friends but then, at the drop of a dime, pull me in and embrace me like he loved me? The pieces didn't fit. He would wait until we were alone in a hall or a room or lagging behind our group of friends just enough to grab me, passionately make out with me, and then walk away immediately like nothing happened, leaving me wanting more, obviously. This was a common behavior for him.

On one side, I thought that maybe it was because we loved differently. I'd second-guess myself thinking maybe his love language wasn't physical touch, but it was. I knew it was. He showed love by doing acts of service for me, little favors here and there, and with physical touch. He would love hard and pull away harder. It was becoming an Olympic-level mind game. Friends never understood because they didn't see the side of him that I saw. I tried bringing it up to a few friends, but since we were so good at laying low with our relationship, they were more eager to catch up and get the details of how we'd been doing than to let me vent and help me clarify. My best friend, Kelsey, had gone into *hate Evan mode*, so I quickly realized that I couldn't talk with her about him because she didn't like him to begin with. She kept saying how much of an arrogant jerk he was. She didn't want me to date him, and she definitely didn't want me to care about our relationship as much as I did. She repeatedly pointed out cute boys and suggested I go talk to them. She wasn't catching on to my lack of interest in her suggestions. I was left to figure out on my own why when we were alone, he'd stare me in the eye like he was going to say exactly what I wanted him to, and instead of words, he'd kiss me, or, worse yet, he'd pull me in closer to him until my body was pressed against his with his gaze locked into mine. I played it over and over again in my head every time it happened, which only made me crave it more. That locked-in gaze—I could stare for hours, and he knew it. He saw me melt in that moment and then came his confident laughter and smile. This devious, I-own-you-but-love-you kind of smile that only he could pull off, it felt like he was laughing at my vulnerability. I couldn't help but wonder if he was as happy in that moment as I was or if this was all just a game to him? After his patented smirk and our bodies touching, he would sometimes even pull away and go about his day like it didn't happen, not even in a tempting way, but almost as if he had changed personalities completely, which of course had me wondering what I had done wrong. Was it my facial expressions or what I said, or did I appear too *melty*? I thought I was good at playing it cool and keeping my withering away as just a secret in my head. Did I turn him off? Or was I overthinking and over critiquing myself while missing the reality of the fact that he just wasn't comfortable in intimate situations? These questions ran through my mind for hours, at night before I fell asleep, and, worse yet, during the day when I should be focusing in class or studying at the coffee shop down the road. He was in my head and taking over.

I wasn't always a doormat beneath him, playing along with his twisted relationship style. There were times when I would say no, either because he had been rude to me that day or crossed a line in another way but putting my foot down was about as effective as a cup with a hole in it. He learned me. He knew me better than I did in some categories of myself. He'd give me a look that shook me as he locked in eye contact with his giant brown eyes. He'd look down at my lips and then go straight for my neck. I mean, come on, how could I turn that down? Give me all of the white towels in the world cause I'm throwing them all in. Where are the forks? Put one in me; I'm done.

I joke about it, but it truly was unfair, the power he had over me. I understand that it was partially my fault and I should have been able to stand my ground and take better control.

It bothered me that I didn't. There were many times when I felt like I was just a convenient hook-up to him—convenient because he knew how to charm me with the snap of his fingers. If this was just friends to him, I knew I loved being his friend, but I wasn't sure I would ever be his girlfriend. I told myself to take a step back and mean it—a real, intentional line between friend and one-hundred-night-stand.

9

Your Loss

We worked a few funerals together as hands-on learning for class credits. Since I was already working for a funeral home, I used them for my case studies and Evan just tagged along to get his credits as well. My bosses loved having Evan as part of the team and told me he was welcome back anytime for more hands-on experience. We were coached on appropriate behavior during the formalities and got to apply the training we were learning in school. I was so thankful we got to do these long hours together because he made working not *work*. We'd catch each other's eye and smile momentarily as if it were just us, when in reality we were in a large room full of people—very emotional, very aware people. We were meant to blend in as if invisible, but Evan in a suit was anything but invisible. He wasn't the type of guy to tailor anything, yet his suit fit him perfectly. It clung to the peaks of his thighs and wrapped around his torso the way I wanted to. I was trying to be near him all day while pretending to only be *accidentally* stalking him all morning. He would go on and on talking about his thoughts, beliefs, and the changes he wanted to make to our industry moving forward. I was mesmerized. He was so driven and so confident in what he wanted and in what he believed to be correct. We had worked our butts off that day, so we were a little sweaty underneath our suits. I was uncomfortable in my suit coat in the slowly warming weather of summer and was so eager to take it off the second we were released from our work duties. When I successfully climbed up into his truck and buckled up for the ride from the cemetery back to the funeral home, my home, my suit coat was history- off and in the back. I was so much more comfortable and relaxed until he threw me off my axis by saying, "Your sweat smells like my mom's sweat."

My jaw nearly hit my lap, and I let out an exhalation that sounded like a chuckle. I didn't know how on earth one would respond to that. *First of all, who says that? And better yet, who thinks that? Is that a normal thing to say?* Not that I needed to come back with a cool quip after being hit with an unusual sentence like that, but I was disappointed in myself for not coming up with something better than "Well, guys always marry their mother. Watch out, Ellis." with an unsmooth wink to follow.

He had nothing to say to my comment, and we drove the rest of the way in near silence. We made it to the parking lot of the funeral home, and he followed me up to my place to help me pack for my weekend trip. I was getting ready to head home to my parents' house for the weekend and had to take a few bags of things back with me. He volunteered to help so I didn't have to carry everything down the stairs on my own.

As he made his last trip down to my car, I used the opportunity to change out of my suit and into comfortable travel clothes. As I stripped down to my bra and underwear, I noticed I forgot to pack my favorite sweatshirt and went across my room to look for it. I heard my apartment door open and him head into the bathroom so I knew I had a little time before he would barge into my room. We were pretty comfortable with each other at that point, and it was mainly because he had a way of claiming me as his own, didn't understand boundaries, and immediately went into our relationship with certain walls down. One of those walls was personal space boundaries. He peed with the door open and once finished, headed straight into my room to find me in my underwear, reaching to the top of my closet for a pair of leggings to pack with the aforementioned sweatshirt.

"You need to gain weight," he said coldly.

My current diet consisted of various cheeses and burritos. I was lucky to have stayed so thin. He made a lot of comments about other people's weight and his own. He, if anything, was underweight; yet he was always so aware of each pound on his body and mine. Even though he was apparently displeased with my frame, I loved it. I was happy with my body and told him not to look at me if he didn't like what he saw. He chuckled as he disregarded what I just said and walked out of my room to let me finish getting dressed. I sounded confident but I didn't feel it. After he left my room, I stared down at my stomach then looked over to see my reflection in my mirror. I too disregarded our conversation and continued to put my clothes on, turn off my bedroom light, and shut the door behind me. When I headed toward him and grabbed my duffel bag filled with clothes, a toothbrush, and more shoes than I probably needed to take with me, he mentioned his lack of weekend plans like he was poking for an invitation.

"Would you like to come with me?" I asked.

He looked at me with the half smile that I loved and politely said, "No, but thank you for offering."

I was surprised he declined and slight bummed because, for the last five seconds, I was eager to show him around my hometown and take him to my favorite restaurant, which had the best views of my tiny local city. I shrugged and said, "Your loss," with a half-smile that tried to mimic his.

He watched me put my duffel bag in my passenger seat, and when I was all set to leave and standing in front of him to say goodbye, he grabbed the shoulder of my shirt that had fallen a few inches and straightened it into place. I got on my tiptoes to wrap my arms around his neck to give him a long hug before leaving for the weekend, super thankful in that moment that I had reapplied my deodorant to avoid smelling like his mom, especially as he was looking into my eyes with a knee-weakening gaze and said, "Don't miss me too much."

It hurt a little bit to drive away as I hoped for the fastest weekend of my life.

10

No Place Like Home

Just when I thought I had everything *in the bag*, I learned that my metaphorical bag wasn't as full as I had hoped. "We've decided to sell the funeral home." The words felt like sandpaper. The owners of the funeral home had a meeting to update the staff of the upcoming changes. There were three of us, so it was a small, informal meeting. We were just attentively looking at the owners from our desks as they told us that they had an offer come in for the funeral home that they were not expecting and since they had talked about retiring in the near future, they couldn't pass up an offer so good. They waited until the sale process was further along and verified that the family was qualified for the purchase before telling us the news so as not to concern us for no reason. It was sad to hear because I adored my bosses. They were ideal. Especially for a girl that was in new territory. They welcomed me with open arms and treated me like I was a part of their family since day one. Gail even brought in gifts for me from time to time just because it made her think of me or seemed like something I would like. Even though I was sad to hear it, I didn't feel that particular sense of fear for my job or discomfort for the change. I adapt well to change and was eager to meet my new bosses until they told me that it was a couple who was newly married and did not have a lot of funding for staff, especially after placing a cushioned offer on a beautiful funeral home. The new owners, Greg and Jeremy, planned to run the funeral home together, just themselves, no staff. There was certainly no room in the budget to pay a student and especially not for the weeks that I didn't work, like my current payroll was formatted—one week on, one week off but paid the same rate weekly along with free, gorgeous housing.

Okay, now I can be worried. I was worried about my financial state since I had just lost my job along with my other coworkers. That wasn't the worst of it yet. Gail told me that Greg and Jeremy would be living in the apartment above the funeral home, where I was currently living. I waited for her to finish that sentence with "But they have a house to sell so you have time and will be able to live here until you graduate" or "But since it's huge and has four bedrooms, you can room with them." However, that was most certainly not the case. "They are planning on moving in on the day of closing since they are staying with Greg's family currently. They sold their house a few months back to help push the purchase of the funeral home."

My stomach churned. I asked how long I had to find a new home. They had an ever-changing timeline and couldn't guarantee a date. They estimated a month or so.

I immediately got in contact with the school to tell them the news and to get an early start on finding another funeral home to get placed into. I remembered them saying when I enrolled and signed up with my funeral home location that I was lucky that they had joined the program late because there weren't any spots left, but I was staying optimistic, hoping that a student had changed his or her mind last minute or wasn't a good fit for the funeral home he or she was placed with and decided to live off-site instead. Nope, that wasn't the case. They apologized through and through for connecting me with a place that only months later had decided to sell and back out of the program. In their defense, there wasn't any obligation to the students. No contract was required, and there weren't any timeline requirements. They were doing me a favor, so they had all the right to sell their business. It was just highly inconvenient for me at the time. I must say, it really helped me keep my mind off of any drama going on with Evan. I couldn't care less about what he was up to, as I was nose to nose with having nowhere to stay and no job to pay for a new place to stay.

The president of the college, Christina, was panicked for me and hit the grindstone looking for alternative options, as did I. I asked about her properties and if any were available in the coming months when the previous class graduated and left their apartments. It was three months away or so, but it was a great location, right next to school and about half the amount of rent that any other apartment half as nice would be in the city.

"The only apartment I have coming available soon is a

two-bedroom, one bathroom, you'd be rooming with Mr. Ellis."

Give me a break. The defeated expression on my face encouraged her to then say, "I know you two are friends, but are you okay living with the opposite sex?"

"I'm not sure." I finally spoke up. I wanted to say, "No, it's not okay. We're on and off more than the lights in here, and I'm really not in the mood to live with the guy, but I'm close to being homeless so I guess I'll lower my standards." What I actually said was "I'll run it past him and see how he feels about it. I'm sure he wouldn't mind having someone to pick up after him" with a polite smile.

On one hand, I was worried about this being my only option, especially since I didn't have a job lined up and my money would only go so far. I was sure to run out of money before the end of the year if I didn't find a job that was flexible with my school schedule and my new full-time job of studying. On the other hand, I couldn't just move in with a guy I was sleeping with—or had been sleeping with. Sound the alarms! That was a recipe for disaster. However, I was over there almost every day with the guys to hang out, and he made it clear he wasn't interested in dating this year. I did have my newfound stand against sleeping with him anymore since I was over his games, so maybe we really could live together. We could possibly make it work; we would just have to be done trying to make *us* work.

We had all talked about it a few times before but with a joking tone since the group of us friends ended up staying there most nights and the guys got tired of sleeping on the floor while his roommate, who was never home, had an empty bed and bare room. I slept comfortably each time I stayed over because I got to curl up in his king-sized bed with him, but the guys couldn't help but dream of putting bunk beds in the spare room and sleeping in there instead of rotating from couch to floor. We came up with different scenarios for bunking there since we felt like we lived there already. Also, getting to live in one of the school's properties would mean that I didn't have to worry as much about working since they charged next to nothing for rent. I could focus my time on balancing studying and hanging out with the guys, which greatly reduced the stress that our high-pressure curriculum caused.

I didn't want to present it to Evan with any bias because I didn't want him to feel pressured. I knew he liked to have his space at times, his quiet nights in, and my people-pleasing side hated putting people in situations where they felt pressured one way or the other. In addition, I would have a rule of my own. If I lived there, we were friends only and not a couple.

Roommates or not, sleeping together wasn't a bridge I planned to cross any time soon because I was being stubborn, and he continued to send me mixed signals. But if we lived in the same apartment, boyfriend and girlfriend titles were off the table for sure. Roommates and friends would be our only titles. As I was driving home from my talk with Christina, the president, Evan called me to ask how my conversation went. Again, I was trying to stay neutral since I saw perks in both outcomes. I wanted to be able to freely let our relationship grow if he decided one day he wanted it to, but more so, I needed to look out for myself and make smart decisions, especially when it came to housing and school. I didn't want to blow an opportunity for a boy. Since it was a hard decision, I wanted to stay neutral and get his opinion. I told him about our conversation and her offer.

He was quiet for a few seconds and then asked, "What do you want to do? How do you feel about that?"

"It's not up to me," I quickly corrected him. "It's your apartment. It's your call." It was Christina's apartment, but I needed to stay neutral.

"Would that work? Isn't that kind of fast?"

"Fast for what?"

"For us, moving in together."

"Well, that brings up my next point. If I lived there, we can't date; we'd be just friends. Also, didn't you say we weren't a couple and you don't want to date? So, what's with your question of if is this fast for us?" I couldn't let that one go.

"You know what I meant."

I didn't.

"I don't know. Let me think about it. When do you need to know?" he said.

"She didn't give me a timeline. I'm guessing sooner rather than later. But take your time and think it through."

- - -

The next day at class, Taylor comes up to me in shock. "Did you really try to move in with Evan already?"

"Whoa, what did he say? I mean, how did he say it? Because even though that's the gist of it, I think he said it out of context." I cringed.

Apparently, Evan was telling a handful of people that I went crazy girlfriend on him and asked to move in with him. I was the butt of many jokes that came firing my way. *I'm homeless. Marry me. Nice to meet you. We should live together.* Fury filled my bones from head to toe. I was so mad at him for twisting the story that I made clear to him as well as calling me his girlfriend when a few days prior, he was not interested in dating and wanted to stay single. Which was it? I could feel my organs vibrating. I was embarrassed that anyone would have believed him and concerned that maybe he didn't understand me correctly, but that couldn't be the case because I really made an effort to make it clear and neutral.

Underneath it all, I had an underlying issue with feeling like I wasn't ever heard. I repeated myself occasionally because I feared the person didn't really hear me. Maybe I should have repeated myself over and over again to Evan in our conversation the day before. Taylor asked how the call actually went and thankfully so because he was able to give Evan a hard time about twisting it while also keeping it playful and light as they usually did. I'm not sure exactly what he said, but I'm certain it contained laughter and none of the vulgar words I pictured using. I was so upset that people were being told anything negative and false about me and digesting it as the truth. That was something I just couldn't handle. I was not one of those people who could proudly say, "I don't care what other people think." I did care, especially when I was being portrayed in the wrong light. I felt the need to shout the truth to everyone so that maybe then they'd understand that I wasn't a forward girlfriend and that I wasn't his girlfriend at all! I wanted to go to every length to clear the air, but it wasn't realistic or really worth my effort. Instead, I needed to bottle all of that effort up for when I confronted Evan trying to figure out what in the heck he was thinking.

I was finally able to corner him and made it even clearer to him than the first time, which was apparently not clear enough. I then added that not only was being roommates not an option in the slightest anymore but that our plans for the night, week, and month were cancelled. I knew that I should have been treated better than that, especially by someone I trusted. I was in a very vulnerable position of not having secure housing in a time of high stress. Everyone needs a place to call home, and mine was slowly slipping out of my grasp. When I reached out for help, I was misquoted, misrepresented, and laughed at. He could have handled that in literally one million other ways.

I was back to square one. I went downstairs to work, feeling defeated from my unsuccessful housing search online and trying to get over my not-boyfriend being a nimrod. My bosses pulled me aside for another meeting for an update on the sale of the funeral home. I went in with selfish hope, only to find out that my one month was cut down to two weeks. I was sick to my stomach but couldn't let it show. Aside from being in my mid-twenties and wanting to pull a dramatic fit like I was feeling inside and let them know my anger toward them—*You don't agree to house a student for a year and then pull the rug out from underneath them*—I knew how you carried yourself carried your reputation, and your reputation carried your career. I took this pile of bad news with another polite grin and fake grace. In reality, I wanted to fetal position myself in the corner and cry, but that wouldn't get me anywhere. I relayed the news to Christina and was so grateful when her face made the expression I was feeling inside. I wasn't alone in thinking I was in between a rock and a hard place – a really dirty rock and a really ugly hard place. She promised to get back to me with some good news. She didn't let me down. I heard back from her a few days later. Their other apartment, which was directly across the street from Evan's apartment, would most likely have a room available because a student who was going to live in it was debating whether or not to start school a year later because of an unfortunate family situation. Was I a bad person for cheering about the possible opening? It only took hours before it was confirmed. I sprinted into her office and signed on the dotted line so quickly that my signature was just a wavy line. It could have been anyone's name at that point. Christina was so excited to tell me about the opening that she actually pulled me out of class to tell me the good news. It was like a breath of fresh air, but it only came after three crying breakdowns and a few pounds of cortisol fat created in my body. As good as this news was, it didn't *totally* solve my problem because the apartment would only be open for the last six months of school. I still had three months left to fill. The hardest part was finding an apartment complex that would allow me to sign a month-by-month lease. They all wanted at least six months. I wasn't willing to give up my apartment right next to the school with rent so cheap I could afford it without any pressure to work while juggling school. I had a list of apartments that I needed to call and tour, so I recruited some friends to join me in the "fun" of it all. When I finally found a place that agreed to a monthly lease, it was of course a very expensive lease and didn't have any upgrades in the unit. They also didn't have a unit open for another month. I was disappointed but remembered a coworker offering to let me stay with her and her sister while I found a place. I was nervous to actually take her up on the offer. I was worried she didn't really mean it and was just being polite, but I was down to just over a week before I needed to be out of the funeral home, and this was my last option on housing, so I took it. I signed the lease that I knew I couldn't afford to stay in for any longer than those two months and cringed at the non-refundable "property care charge."

I went into work the next day and arrived at the same time as Olivia, the coworker who had so generously offered me her spare room. I was eager to talk to her but didn't want to bombard her in the parking lot. We no sooner made it through the second set of glass doors than the owners walked toward us with stone-cold faces. They said the buyers needed to move in that weekend and would be taking over at that point, which was in three days. We both were getting hit with heavy information. I was three days from homeless and really needed to talk to the girl beside me about living with her for a month, but she had just been told that she was losing her job in three days, so I stayed silent. I didn't fake smile, and I didn't say, "No worries, I'll figure it out!" There was no fake grace left in me at this point. The four of us just stared off while in each other's company. The owners were sad as well because this funeral home had been passed down through their family for years. They were the fourth generation to own it and didn't focus on saying goodbye to that legacy with the mess of the sale, and they were hit with the reality of it all at once. Olivia spoke first, bless her generous freaking heart. She turned her head to me and said, "Please stay at my place for a while. I know you don't have anywhere to go this soon. Stay as long as you need."

I felt a heavy wave of relaxation roll over my body and teared up. "You don't know how much that means. Thank you … truly."

***

Evan and another friend, Justin helped me move my

things from the funeral home to Olivia's house. Yes, Evan. He came over a few nights after our argument about the roommate situation. I didn't want to unlock the door to let him in, but he had this unfortunate pull over me so I had the door open within ten seconds of his knock. I wanted to be mad at him. I had so much anger built up for him, and this really hurt me so it was the perfect ammunition to ride this argument out until I was able to get him to see the damage his heavy words could make. I started off across the room from him at the other side of the kitchen island, but one plea after another, I was standing within arm's reach of him.

"I didn't think it would snowball like it did. I just didn't know how to react to that conversation."

"I could have come up with about fifty better ways for you to have handled it."

"I'm sure you could have, but you're better with communicating how you feel and what's in your head. I'm not. I never have been. If we're going to ever work, you need to be okay with that."

I went into defense mode and immediately started prying. "I know you aren't great at communicating, but you had no problem communicating our conversation to everyone you came across that day. What's your excuse for that?"

"I shouldn't have told anyone. I get that now, but I wanted to get it off my chest and get ideas on how my friends would handle being in that situation. It's not my fault they're all gossips."

He had a point. The school was essentially a sardine can full of gossip. As if there wasn't enough on our plates, they needed to add more by digging into classmates' lives? It was beyond me. Again, one of those topics I won't waste my time delving deeper into.

Evan and I talked it out, and I forgave him. I didn't forget by any means, but I forgave. I kind of needed him. I needed *us* during this time. With all the crazy going on around me, I needed to know I had a safe place—a home. Through all of the moving and the stress and the mess, he was my home, my safe spot I wanted to be curled up into.

- - -

I went from a large apartment to a bedroom, and I wasn't a light packer, so most of my things went in their garage. I was so grateful to have a place to stay. They embraced my company, and their house was so cute! It looked like an Ikea showroom and smelled like a bakery. Olivia loved to decorate, bake, and cook. I was in temporary heaven. They had a dog and two cats, and I loved them instantly. I spent my nights on the couch, drinking wine with the girls after taking their dog for a walk together. I never asked Evan to come over because it wasn't my house, and I knew he would never be interested in meeting two new people and hanging out watching chick flicks, which I understood. I spent a lot of time and nights over at Evan's because it felt more like home to me even though nothing but my toothbrush and favorite wine were over there. I had to bring my clothes for the next day every time I stayed and just ended up using his shampoo and, dare I say it, skipped the conditioning portion of my routine. The bottle said two-in-one, but my hair disagreed. Nonetheless, I preferred to shower at his place. We would "save water," as he called it, and shower together, which, let's be honest, is always more fun than showering alone.

Despite him making it very clear that he didn't want me to live with him, he sure loved having me over. He bought me almond milk when he was at the store so I would have something to eat my cereal with and always had apples in the kitchen, my favorite kind of course. He even kept them in the refrigerator because I prefer them cold. It doesn't seem like much in the big picture, but in the moment, knowing he thought of me when I wasn't around made me feel so loved and spoke to me in a way that no words could. I still spent nights at the girls' house because Evan was big on having his space every now and then and I was too. I needed some time to decompress and just really let loose in my old, torn sweatpants. Even though I was so fortunate to be staying with Olivia and her sister, and even though they said how happy they were to have me stay there, I couldn't help but feel like an intruder occasionally and started being very aware of how many days I had left until I was in my own apartment. I wanted to walk around in my underwear and blare music while I showered. I noticed myself counting down the days in increments of halves: fourteen and a half days, fourteen days, thirteen and a half days …

11

Short Lived

The feeling of being in my own place was exactly what I had been needing. There were so many uncertainties in my life at this moment that I needed a constant. The constant was that I would get to live here for the next two months. I knew who would be there and when because it was *my* space- I once again had my own home. If I left something on the counter when I left for class in the morning, it would be in the same spot when I got home. This wouldn't last for long; I knew that when my two months here were up, that I would have a roommate and my moments of full control were few. I soaked them up while they lasted. I also soaked up the view of Evan and his latest fling while he flirted with her – out in the open- in the hallway at school. Why was I the only one that he kept a secret? He was pretty obvious with the others.

I needed some time away from Evan and since Kelsey wouldn't leave me alone about dating and seeing what else was out there, I hung out with a guy that worked at the same funeral home as Taylor. His name was Theo and he looked like a preppy lumberjack with a long beard and even longer, wavy dark hair that ended just past his shoulders but spent more time up in a loose bun. He wore fitted jeans and plaid shirts with the sleeves perfectly rolled up to his forearms. We met when he came over to Taylor's to hang out. The two of them together were a riot. They both wrestled in high school so repeatedly put each other in some sort of "hold" in a slew of inopportune times. They had their fair share of inside jokes and laughed endlessly at them and practically finished each other's sentences. How many credit hours was Taylor logging at this funeral home? It seemed more like he was just hanging out there continually and becoming best friends with this lumberjack guy. Theo had a perfect black Labrador puppy named Luna and he brought her with him everywhere. He asked me, right in front of Evan and Taylor if I wanted to join him on their walk. "Sure, I'd love to." I said, as Evan's face tightened. I wanted to look him right in the eye and ask how his own medicine tasted but I took the more mature, quieter route against my impulse. So, Theo, Luna and I took a long walk through the trails nearby. Even after hours of walking up and down trails, he smelled so good, I can still remember it. Like a mixture of cologne and leather. Whether we were together or just texting, he said all the right things. He registered as a solid ten out of ten and I liked him. We hung out a few times and I enjoyed every second. On paper, he was perfect, but I wanted him to be Evan and he wasn't. I tried to move on and focus on the great qualities of the many men in this large city, but I was always pulled back to Evan. We just fit better together- like a favorite old sweatshirt that you know you should toss but it fits so well and is so comfortable, that was Evan to me.

Understanding the importance of a good fit, I spent a decade looking for the right pair of denim shorts, a pair that didn't make me hate my body or break my budget. I'm convinced that denim hates the female population, and only a few of us are able to trick it on occasion when we find the perfect pair. I like the look of denim, but it was by no means reciprocated. I wear my denim jacket every chance I get but immediately regret it minutes later when I'm reminded for the seven hundredth time how uncomfortable it is. The same goes for jeans and shorts. They either don't fit my butt or my thighs or are too big around my waist, leaving that sagged opening right above my butt. Well, I had finally found my pair of denim shorts. Praise! They were dreamy. They fit like a glove and were the right amount of frayed that I could take them from day to night. I could sit down in them without the leg hole cutting into my thigh, and they were on sale, so the price was just right. I wore these shorts as much as socially acceptable, so of course I was wearing them when I went over to Evan's for date night.

- - -

Evan has this Christian Grey side to him that he loved to bring out more often than not. You would think he watched the movie on repeat like every single day, but I digress. He was on his A game that night and was saying all the right things. I was putty in his hands, as per usual. We were making late-night snacks in his kitchen when he grabbed me at the height of the back of my thighs, and his hands slipped right under and into the bottom of my shorts to lift me onto the countertop. He had apparently lost interest in the homemade potato chips, and it all went onto me. He flipped the Christian Grey switch and went full "do you trust me?" while I teetered on the edge of where the counter met the sink. Never once did he break eye contact. He didn't even hesitate before leaning in for a long and heated kiss. From that point on, it only escalated. Things were falling into the sink behind me, and I nearly did too when he bit my shoulder. I was used to his affectionate nibbles, but this was a bite, so I jumped and slapped his arm in return, only breaking the moment for a second. He didn't skip a beat. He just gave that look I craved and went right back to kissing me. I felt his hands on my new jean shorts, then I heard denim ripping. I tried to look down, but he pulled my chin up and directed my lips back to his. Part of me cared about him tearing my new, favorite jean shorts, but the majority of me didn't. I was absorbed in this moment and didn't want anything to ruin it, especially not a quick fix from a seamstress. He hadn't unbuttoned them, but his hand was in them, and it didn't quite add up, even in my love-drunk stupor. I looked down to see a very long rip and immediately laughed in disbelief while backhanding his chest.

"What the hell, Ev?"

"You're fine."

"Yeah, I am, but my shorts aren't."

"Shut up about your shorts, or I'll rip them the whole way."

I shot him a look that I can only describe as pissed, but I was trying not to laugh, which took us out of the Christian Grey moment and into a more "us" moment of laughing and play-wrestling, leading us right back into the heat of the moment. I must have made additional comments about the shorts because they were now shredded on his floor. I grabbed them quickly to show him the destruction he'd made on our way into his bedroom. The only emotion he showed was pride. I wanted him to feel remorseful, but instead, it gave him fuel- we had our best sex that night. I woke up in his king-sized bed with tousled sheets and the sun peeking through the blinds—no Evan though. He had beaten me to the living room and was lounged back in his recliner. He sat there looking half-awake with his coffee in hand and eyes glued to the TV. I went back into his room, opened his bottom drawer, and grabbed his white basketball shorts to wear home since mine were done for. When I walked out to kiss him goodbye before my much-needed shower, the first words out of his mouth were "Why did you take my shorts?" with his palm in the air as if telling me to stop in my tracks.

"Seriously? You destroyed mine in the kitchen last night. I need something to wear home."

"No, technically, you destroyed them. I told you not to bring them up again, or I'd rip them more. Yet, you kept blabbering about them being torn, so I finished the job. If you would have shut up about it, you'd still have half of them."

"And what would I do with half a pair of shorts? You know what? No, I'm not even addressing your nonsense. I can't go home half naked so I'm taking these."

"But those shorts? They're my favorite. I'll never get them back."

I held up my denim scraps and smirked with defiance.

"Yeah, well, these were my favorite, and I'll never get them back."

As the door shut behind me, I chuckled because I could hear him continuing the debate. I didn't really win though. He came over the next day and stole them from my dryer. He got his shorts back, and I still don't have mine. If he was trying to mark his territory, to remind me that I was under his thumb, he did a damn good job at it.

12

Blurred Lines

I was beginning to see traits of myself that didn't exist before I knew Evan. They existed only because I wanted to be the perfect girlfriend for him, or non-girlfriend, whatever I was at the time. All I wanted was to validate myself to him, to prove to him that I was worthy of his time. The real problem is that I felt like I needed to prove that to him. When I would receive praise for something I'd accomplished, such as make it into Pi Sigma Eta, a fraternity based on academic standing, I wanted him to know. I didn't want to celebrate with him, I wanted to prove to him that others saw my value and he should too. I put a lot of this pressure on myself, and it was all fueled by him. What hurt the most was when he didn't care. I wanted to crawl into a hole when he would follow up my excitement with critique and criticism: "I was eligible also, but I turned it down. It doesn't mean anything in the real world, it's a waste of your time" "I don't like those jeans," or "You're going to fix your hair before we go, right?" It made me feel so small and insignificant.

Although his wounding words brought me down, I would prefer him to come out and say what he was thinking or wanting instead of keeping it in and lying to me. Regardless of being hurt, without fail, I would melt like butter when he mixed a sultry look into my eyes and a soft sweep through my hair. I couldn't do anything in those moments except stare up at him in discontent. Even though my body was putty, my stare was firm. I knew he could see that he made a mistake and frayed the string holding us together because he began to apologize. I forgave him, every time.

Some of the things he said had a forceful push even though they were delicate words. His mannerisms, body language, and words didn't always match each other. On top of all the confusion in his communication style were the quirks that made his words memorable. He had a little accent in his voice, but it was more of an unnoticed roll under his words. His r's lingered longer, and his n's were more pronounced than mine. Because it was a word that he said so often and because it showed off his accent so much, *drunk* is the perfect word to describe it. He pronounced it as if the r and n were accented harder—dRuNk. He blamed his mindless actions and hurtful words on his alcohol intake, being dRuNk, and promised me that outside of our stressful atmosphere of school, he was a different person, a much better person. I wanted to see it. Well, I wanted to *experience* it. I could *see* it. I imagined him as his best self and focused on his potential. I got tastes of it. It was the guy I spent time with one on one, the one who told me how much he loved having my hand in his because of the way they fit so perfectly.

"I always worried that I had small hands, but they fit in yours perfectly," he said as we laid together on his large leather couch. He had insecurities and worries but they were overshadowed by his soft heart. I heard how much he valued his family in the stories he told me as we laid together, just talking. He would do anything for any one of them, and I knew once I was in that circle that I would be his priority—or one of the top ones at least.

I wasn't grasping at straws. I had a great guy. I was willing to love him *as is* and was only more excited about him being an even better, more loving, more caring version of himself. I was afraid of one day not being the lucky one who got to witness him grow up and mature. I didn't put all this time and effort in, along with the emotional and physical roller-coaster ride, to give up halfway through. I was all in. I'd pictured it; we'd be living up north, maybe in Wisconsin, running a funeral home together. I'd have a little garden in the backyard of our two-story house we were renovating. There'd be a swing set already in the backyard for when that special day came that we got to start our family. I could picture his beaming, tear-filled smile paired with nervous laughter as we made eye contact when I walked down the aisle toward him in the church he grew up in, surrounded by our family and friends—but not too many because we were more "small wedding" kind of people. We would write our own vows, and they would be about our journey up until that point and how we had unknown journeys ahead of us, but we were ready for whatever life handed us because we knew, together, we could get through it all. I needed this daydream to come to fruition one day.

Our friends brought up our future wedding just as much as they jumped back and forth on whether they were for us or against us. They called me Mrs. Ellis and had their own plans about the speeches they would give at our wedding and the stories they would tell our children one day about how their mom and dad had met and embarrassed themselves and maybe use a few stories as blackmail for years later. I knew it was further along in the future but thinking about it gave me so much joy I couldn't help myself but daydream.

Despite our ups and downs, he told me I was an easy target. He wasn't wrong. My kryptonite was dancing in the kitchen. We would sway together even with no music, no noise, just silence, nothing but my nervous giggle and his "got you" chuckle with his left hand cupping my right hand, my head leaning on his chest at the perfect height to hear his heart beat a little faster until he would push me out and into a spontaneous spin and dip. We danced as smoothly as if we did it daily. Nothing of talent but we were connected and in sync. He used this tactic when he wanted to get his way or make up for something that he had done wrong. He knew it made me vulnerable. Once my walls were down, he'd kiss my neck and leave me wanting more—more kissing, more self-control, more moments like these, more commitment, more from him, and more from myself to know that this was it and that there wouldn't be more no matter how often I wished for it. The truth was I didn't know if I could handle more.

- - -

Our love was only manageable in small doses. A little

bit here and a little bit there. Too much time together was unhealthy for both of us, as if our being together dripped trace amounts of gasoline onto a fire, and eventually it would get too out of control to manage. I learned about the love between Frida Kahlo and Diego, and ever since then, I can't help but compare us to them, possibly because in everyday life, we didn't really better each other. We had many conversations about deep and heavy topics. We'd debate opinions and give each other motivating advice or lend a listening ear when the other had a problem. Even still, we destroyed each other in a wonderful way. Our friends begged us to stop dating and just remain friends—nothing more. They were tired of playing referee and witnessing us breaking into fights and then making out in his kitchen moments later. I can't blame them. They didn't see us in our prime because our prime was when it was just he and I, when he could let his guard down and be open with me. Maybe they would have understood why what we had was worth fighting for.

The picturesque love scene of looking into each other's eyes and not seeing anyone else in the room wasn't us. We were very aware of the others in the room, or at least he was very aware of them. He kept secrets from all of them, secrets about his vulnerable side, his emotions, and his heart. Our entire relationship felt like he was hiding it from everyone. I put so much effort into being his perfect girl but instead became his perfectly kept secret.

13

Broken

Spoiler alert. He broke my heart again. I kept telling myself it was fine, and that it was just the same idea of *kintsugi*, an age-old method of repairing broken pottery with powdered gold because the golden lines added beauty to the piece. It was the idea of taking something broken and making it more valuable. This was essentially the state of my heart at this point. It was broken time and time again, but each time, I learned something new about how I loved and how I wanted to be loved in return, making my heart only more valuable than it was before.

As much as I knew I shouldn't go back to him because friends told me time and time again that I would be making a huge mistake and would just get hurt again, I went back. I knew what would happen, but I still wondered if maybe it wouldn't this time and was still surprised every time history repeated itself. Like putting a Mentos into a bottle of soda—you know what's going to happen; you've seen it before. Their chemicals are going to react, and an explosion will occur because those two forms of matter can't exist in the same container. There's too much pressure, and they explode, messily. We were just that—messy. My index finger and thumb would have a tight grip on the Mentos knowing that I should pivot to the right and set the Mentos down, yet my thumb and index finger released the tension and slowly separated until the Mentos fell right into the soda. I looked intently, watching the explosion as it flowed over the edge of the glass and spilled down my recently cleaned counter down to my recently mopped floor, creating the same exact mess I cleaned up moments earlier. It never had a different reaction. Neither did I. Time and time again, I was ready and willing to clean up the mess and then make it all over again.

In my defense, he had a smile that would stop anyone in their tracks. A smile that, alone, was worth going back to. In fact, we got stopped a lot by people telling him he had a beautiful smile. He would shut down immediately when someone complimented him. I expected him to blush like I would if someone complimented me, but he didn't; he did the opposite. His smile just stopped in its tracks, disappeared, and became a closed-mouth grin with a shy "thank you" before he walked away, trying to avoid the situation altogether. I hadn't seen a person so afraid of a compliment. At times, he could be the toughest guy I knew, and then other times, he would shrink himself down as small as he could get. Trying to get him to smile in photos was a tough job. The whole "say cheese" charade meant to him that he needed to close his mouth more tightly. I have so many pictures with him just giving the camera a grin. Only on my most persuasive days could I capture one of him giving me the smile I loved. He opened up to me about it and told me that he didn't want to come off as a pretty boy or like he needed compliments from people. He wanted to be taken seriously. I was confused about how and why he put so much concern around something as simple as a smile. I understood being taken seriously but only when at work or in a stern argument. Being too serious in everyday life was boring. Again, this nonsensical lecture was coming from a guy who continually said how he just wanted to have fun and relax, so why the flood of hypocrisy?

In another one of his shining, hypocritic moments, he had the nerve to tell me that I broke his heart and hurt him when I went on a date with someone else, but he was sleeping with three other girls. Why couldn't I just walk away from him? At this point, I knew he was interested in other girls. He was not cheating on me because we weren't together, but it still felt like it. I constantly wondered why he would rather spend his nights or even days with these other girls instead of me. How did they get his attention more than I did? They didn't though, not *more*. They could catch his attention, but no one could keep it. He lost interest too easily. He had little "flings" here and there, but then he would run back to me long enough for someone to catch his attention again. Then he would pick a fight, and we would break up again. But he kept coming back again, as did I. There wasn't anything he could do or say that would permanently turn me off to him.

I did hate his occasional immaturity. It reminded me of why I refused to date a younger guy for so long. Taylor was only an instigator to the immaturity in Evan, which at times made me hate Taylor. The two of them would give me a hard time anytime I went on a date or talked to someone in the hallway for longer than five minutes. "Did you sleep with him?" or "You came home late last night." They would make one-liner jokes and repeat them over and over and over again until I snapped. Of course, then I was the bad guy for snapping and *why couldn't I just take a joke?* At first, I stood up for myself and made it clear that they were wrong and that I wasn't like that, not the type of girl to sleep with just anyone and especially not that quickly, which was a hard sell considering I had slept with Evan on our first date. He didn't realize he was the exception to the rule, not the rule. That was a common problem with him—him being the exception. I got tired of defending myself for talking with a male student in the hallway to discuss the arterial system in the brain and its cooperation with formaldehyde or whether Wendy's chicken nuggets were better than Chick-fil-A's. Somehow, Evan and Taylor confused that for sex. After a while, it got old and annoying, so I stopped defending myself or trying to untwist their assumptions. It wasn't worth the energy. I started replying to them with "Yup, sure did, just now in the hall" or by saying nothing and just walking past them with an eye roll. It was an easier route than fighting with them about it, especially since I was mentally exhausted from classes and the Evan drama that came along with it all.

None of the drama I experienced with Evan came even close to the mess I experienced with Scott and Leah, especially Scott. We had all grown close like a family instead of friends. Scott had broken up with Leah and was taking it pretty hard. His family was worried about him because of his history with mental illness and suicide attempts in the past and told me their concerns along with giving me the cell phone numbers to pretty much the entire family tree. I was confident I wouldn't ever need to use them but accepted them graciously. He had been supportive in my fifty-seven breakups with Evan, and since I was also friends with Leah and wanted to reconnect the two of them, I was all in on being supportive for him in this time. Scott and Leah lived together, so I told her I would let him stay on my couch until they smoothed things over or worse, until they decided officially that he needed to get his own place.

He was so upset, crying frequently and begging her to let him come home. He had cheated on her in a moment of weakness with a girl he met out one night. I was so mad at him for breaking Leah's heart that I was proud of her for saying no and standing her ground. I would never say that to him of course because my main role at this time was just to be his supporter. He refused to go to classes for a few days, which really put him behind. I made the additional effort to copy my notes and make two sets of everything I did so that he would at least have the material needed when his brain was able to absorb the information. Knowing that he was falling behind in a course where every hour in every day mattered added stress for him.

There was a lot of talking and crying going on in my one-bedroom apartment. He turned my living room into a combination of bachelor pad and tornado victim. I updated his family to keep them in the loop, understanding their concerns. He was starting to come around to himself again after a few days but still refused to go to classes. I was pleased to see that my living room was picked up after day five, so I made him cookies as a thank-you and a boost-up snack. We sat on old stools that I hand painted back in high school around my small kitchen island, eating cookies straight from the oven so hot that he made a joke about the noises we both made trying to cool them off while they were in our mouths like dragons trying to breathe fire but not quite knowing how to. He finally laughed, and I was proud of him for letting his sadness go and appearing ready to get back into his routine again. The night went on with more quality time and a few more cookies paired with cheap wine to wash them down. We said cheers to what was next to come … not knowing what was next to come.

- - -

Hours later into the night, I woke up to knocking on my bedroom door. With one eye half opened, I shouted, "What?" with no intention of moving.

"Nel, I'm going home to see Leah."

Okay, both eyes were open now. "What? Now? Isn't it the middle of the night?"

"Yeah, but she said I could come home. Come lock your door behind me."

I never gave him a key in a small nod to prevent him staying for too long or losing it, knowing him. Against my will, I got up and shuffled to open my bedroom door and follow him to my apartment door. "Thank you for being my best friend, I love you so much," he said with tearful eyes as he gave me a hug.

"Always, you know I have your back through everything. Good luck with Leah. Let me know how it goes—but in the morning," I said with a wink.

He smirked with one side of his mouth and tears in his eyes.

He's so happy now, he even has tears in his eyes— so sweet, I thought to myself as I headed back into my warm bed.

- - -

What felt like seconds later, I woke up to my phone vibrating repetitively. *Scott's dad? Why is his dad calling me at two—*my stomach dropped. What did I just do? Weren't those happy tears? I immediately called him back.

He was sobbing into the phone. "Where did he go?"

"He said he was going home. Leah told him to come home."

"No, she didn't. I just talked with her because … he …"

He couldn't talk anymore, and he passed his phone to Scott's mom, who finished his sentence for him. "He just called us to say goodbye, and we don't know where he is."

"*What?*" I shrieked back.

He seemed fine. He was happy again! None of this made sense. Where did he go? I thought I was going to throw up, and between the nonstop ringing of my phone and talking to each and every one of his family members at different times on the phone to try to track him down and figure out where in the hell he went, I ended up pacing around my apartment, waiting for my phone to ring again until I glanced down at the open and empty bottle of acetaminophen in my bathroom garbage can. I immediately hung up the ringing phone, trying to get ahold of his brother, in order to call his dad, who I knew would answer in one ring, to tell him. "My Acetaminophen bottle is empty! It was full." I rarely take medication. I had it on hand for unruly periods and had taken two out of that bottle at the most, the bottle that was now empty and in my garbage can.

No one could get ahold of Scott. He wouldn't answer his phone for any of his family. I had the idea to play good cop and send him a text that said, "How is it going with Leah?! I want details! I'm too excited for you guys to sleep now lol"—the most insincere "lol" ever sent via text. I knew he wouldn't text back, but my plan was that it would lower suspicion for when I called him minutes later. It didn't work. He didn't answer. I was calling his mom to update her that I hadn't heard from him either when my phone rang. I yelled, "It's him!" and switched over to answer.

"Hey!" I didn't know what the hell to say, and I didn't want to yell and scare him away.

He was slurring his words and making zero sense.

"Where are you? Didn't you go home?"

Without answering my question, he went right into "I can't do it. I'm done. I can't live without her. I'm ending—"

The loudest crash cut off his sentence. I learned later he drove right off the road, all the while never hanging up. I heard everything. I heard the crash and the airbags deploy. I heard him moaning in pain in the background and then later sirens. I wanted so badly to call his parents, but I wouldn't dare hang up. I needed to know where he was and if he was okay so that I had something to tell them. Based on the conversation I could hear, he was unresponsive. I heard the cop connecting to dispatch for an ambulance and giving the general location. I knew then I could hang up and call his parents so they could rush to the scene if possible. I was shaking so badly that my body was twitching. Did I just hear one of my best friends commit suicide? Was I really sending his parents to the scene of it? I didn't know the right thing to do in the moment. I was just taking it step by step.

He was alive. He was in the intensive care unit until

he was stable enough to be transferred to the psych ward for a long-term stay. I was a wreck for the next few days. His family asked me not to tell anyone what had happened until they called the rest of the family, but everyone was asking where Scott was. Every time someone brought it up, I couldn't help but cry. I had to immediately reassure them that Scott was okay. He couldn't have many visitors because of the nature of the collision. So only his large family, Leah, and I went to visit. I was drained and literally felt like the color gray. I still studies and pushed to keep up with my continuing classes in an uncomfortable hospital chair next to my best friend, whom I wanted so badly to live so that I could punch him square in the face.

- - -

Once I got the go-ahead from Scott's mom, later in the day following the crash, I was able to tell the friend group. We visited in groups once the hospital approved additional visitors. Evan never went with us to visit him. "He's doing this for attention, and I refuse to feed into it."

It was not the reaction I expected, but then again, why was I shocked that Evan took the flight path? We were both notorious for choosing flight when it came to the tension response of fight or flight. I told him everything about that night, as Scott's family expected me to. They wanted his friends to be aware and stay open about this time in their lives, but they too didn't expect his reaction. He was nothing short of pissed and annoyed. There wasn't any sympathy in his eyes. I had never seen him so upset while being so cold. I'd seen him upset, of course—at me, at his family (perks of working with them I suppose), and at the workload given by school, but his upset was fueled by his passion for the subject. This time was different. He had gone cold; it was just pure hate. So much so that I wondered if there was an underlying reason. Why did this seem to strike a raw nerve? It took hours of prying and him shutting me out before he finally got out that he was upset for me, for Scott's family, and for Leah having to deal with Scott's "selfish, attention-seeking behavior." "He put you in the middle, scared you, and put you in a position that made you feel any bit of responsibility for his care. He had no right to have you on the phone. You don't deserve to hear that shit. What the fuck was he thinking? Overdosed on pills or not. Penelope, I can't forgive him. I won't ever be able to." He never did.

- - -

Still to this day, he gets so angry when I talk about Scott or Leah. He blocked them both out of his life immediately. Part of me was jealous that he could turn it off so quickly. I wanted to shut them out too, if only to give me a second to heal. It hurt me to look at them or talk to them because I remembered it all. My lungs would feel like they were shaking again, and the sickness in my stomach took weeks to go away. I couldn't eat or sleep without the thought of waking up to his knock or my phone ringing. With the nature of our major, days after his attempt, without the professor knowing, we covered suicide victims and how their bodies would react differently to the embalming chemicals as well as the restorative process to repair their post suicide appearance for the comfort of the family. It was too much at once. I flashed back to the visual of him in the emergency room bed looking worse than I pictured and knowing, based on the material covered, how a funeral director would have taken care of his body had his efforts been successful. I couldn't turn it off.

Against the wish of my gut, I supported him and was there for him until he was released from the mandatory stay in the mental institution. After his release and as he recovered, I pulled away slowly. I couldn't be wrapped up in their world anymore. It wasn't healthy for me. I knew the importance of mental health and self-care in that moment, more so than ever before, and had to take care of myself now.

Evan wasn't much help in the slow pull back. He immediately avoided Scott like he was the living, breathing Ebola virus walking around. He couldn't understand why I wouldn't just cut them off cold like he had. I explained myself for hours, but it never sank in. Although Evan was showing me a combination of his protective side and his unforgiving side, it didn't feel supportive, nor did it feel like what I needed at that moment. He was such a stubborn guy. He was hard-headed with strong beliefs. He wasn't helping me heal from the pain and memories on my end. I needed to talk about it with him and explain how I felt, but he didn't want to hear a word about Scott, so he would stop me seconds after I started. I know he was trying to help me, but he wasn't doing it in a way that was best for me or the way my mind worked. It worked best for his needs and was inconsiderate of mine. He had started to pull away from Scott weeks earlier when he'd cheated on Leah because we were close with her too by association. Evan would get all high and mighty, preaching morality and loyalty, and I couldn't do anything but tip my head as far to the right as it would go as I tried to believe him.

14

My Cup of Sugar

I moved into one of the school's apartments that Christina reserved for me. The apartment was right across the street from Evan's. We could go back and forth to each other's apartments as often as we wanted to. My new home was also right next to the school and more updated than Evan's. It was perfect. Of course, it would then be harder to avoid Evan when he pissed me off, but it would be ideal for when he decided he wanted to be back together again. Our relationship exhausted me, it was a draining roller coaster with the highest peaks and deepest valleys going at an unsafe speed. To some, the rush is addictive, and to others, it's unsettling, and they know to get off the ride immediately.

I was certainly in the former category. I've tried cigarettes and had my fair share of alcoholic drinks, but my attitude toward it all is "in moderation"—until now with Evan. It was clear, even to me that, I was addicted to him. I couldn't get enough of him. It didn't matter how much I got or how much he wrecked me, I wanted more at every chance I could get. Was he addicted to me in return? I worried that he liked to pull me in and then drop me, just to experiment and see if he could and that he was addicted to the game of it and not to me. Continually going back to him let him know that I would always be there, no matter what. That gave him the confidence boost he needed in the moment. Even before Evan, I had always been the one in the relationship to give more and love harder. I remembered details and went out of my way to please people but then got a roller coaster in return. He had his tricks to wrap me around his finger one day and intentionally crush me the next. Was it because he liked seeing how it broke me? Did he like seeing how much he could mean to someone? Did it validate that someone could love him? He had this power over me to play me at his convenience, and then when he needed another fix, I was there for him to do it all over again. Now, being within walking distance of each other, was a whole new loop in this roller coaster. It hurts to remember the heartbreak I felt knowing that before him, I had been so strong and would never used to let a guy run me the way I let Evan. Where did that girl go?

- - -

As much as I want more out of my past self, I understand her completely. Nothing compared to Evan's touch. It gave me a high and a comfort at the same time. I wanted to hold on to those moments that we had together and remember the passion and fire behind them. When we lay together on the couch or shared his favorite old recliner, we had a gentle touch toward one another. It was soft and delicate when he rubbed my arm and kissed my shoulder. We laced our fingers together and pulled each other in close. When we had sex, we turned into a different couple. It was rough and had pressure behind the touching, like we were trying to push through a brick wall together. It was full force, and I craved it. I would walk away with bruises, scratches, and red marks on my body. I even got a hickey from him once and felt like a high schooler. Our bodies shouldn't be able to get hickeys when we reach a certain age, just for the preservation of our dignity. My friends would comment on my marks as if he were abusing me, but he wasn't, not by any means. It was very mutual, which sounds bizarre, but in the moment, when I was halfway up his wall with only his sweat-misted arms holding me up, I'd be lying if I said I wasn't absorbed in the moment and agreeing to more. Since I didn't have anything to hide, I told my friends a brief overview of how I got the marks in question. The first few times, I received a shocked look followed by supportive jealousy, then followed by interest and confusion. As time went on, they began to question him again.

"What an ass."

"Tell him to calm down."

"He needs to reel it in."

They weren't wrong, five or so "battle wounds" were too many and I believe girls and guys need to be aware of taking care of themselves in those situations. Just because I was comfortable in these moments doesn't mean the next person will be or should be. A good portion of the incidents were accidentally self-inflicted by my uneasiness getting the best of me and my coordination. I found myself being clumsy and not my former graceful self when he talked to me. My clumsiness had even sent me to urgent care one night to get a chemical eye-rinse after accidentally using nail polish remover instead of my eye makeup remover. In my defense, they both had purple caps and similar bottles. I was flustered because he was flirting with me via text and laying it on thick. I wanted to get my bedtime routine done so I could lie in bed and enjoy his attention. That's not at all what happened. I set my phone down while trying to come up with a great response for him. My mind was wandering, and I began what I believed to be a mindless task. Seconds later, I had the left side of my face submerged in the running water from my bathroom sink faucet. Next step, once the burning hadn't subsided, was to politely ask my sweet roommate for a ride to urgent care so that I could get an eye flush. "Also, could you please take me like this very second?" I said while staring at her in her pajamas through my one good eye.

The doctor of course questioned me about my mental state and if I had been experiencing any depression or wishes to harm myself. I rolled my eye, my one good eye, and explained that it was an honest mistake in a flustered state. After being further questioned about my flustered state, I tried to explain how I melted and really couldn't function fully when I spoke to this specific guy. The look he gave me made me aware of how crazy I sounded. Maybe if it had been a female doctor she would have understood, or maybe if I didn't continue to let this guy have such reign over me then this would be a nonissue. No one can possibly drive you crazy forever though, right? I assumed it would get better. I mean, how long could these butterflies possibly last?

15

Us And The Sun

As if living across the street wasn't close enough for him, he wanted more time together. He asked me to go on a vacation with him, just the two of us, on a getaway from the stress and the daily routines that were wearing us down. In general, it would be a break from real life. He had asked me to go with him many times before, but I always brushed it off, assuming he was experiencing stress-induced wanderlust that would last only a while. As it turns out, I was wrong about it only being a temporary urge. He found an Airbnb right on the beach; it was very cute with beachy-style decorations. It was unlike him to take initiative like that. He had taken initiative a time or two before but not with something as big as a vacation—a big cue he was eager to go. He took me out to lunch to tell me about the great places he'd found for us to stay in and how good it would be for us to get away for a few days.

"I want to relax and only focus on us and the sun," he said persuasively.

Us and the sun. It had a nice ring to it. It was a great condo in a prime location just South of the Texas border. My schedule was swamped though, and there was no realistic way for me to get away for a day, let alone five of them. I considered blacking out my calendar to whatever date he chose when I envisioned us there in the water and on the beach chairs. What would an oasis like that be like with him? Just Evan and I, no friends around for days. I would get to see his romantic side nonstop. There would be no turning it off and on.

- - -

There was something so tempting about going away together, and being outdoors together for five whole days that made it impossible to say no. Our favorite date activities were all based outside. I think it was because of his energetic nature. He loved to be on the move, outside and golfing especially. If you gave him a golf club or basketball, he would be busy for hours. I decided to take him up on his offer. It was on the water, and somewhere warm. It checked all the boxes. We stayed in a beautiful room with views of the lake. We spent all day out on the dock and in the water, just floating and relaxing while we ignored all of the stresses from school. It was just the two of us under the warm sun, drinks in hand and the day to ourselves. We dove in deeper and talked about our upbringing and our childhood friends, and he told me all about his original career passion to be a science teacher. I thought it was sweet that he opened up to communicating so much. He wasn't always this approachable for long periods of time back home at school. I soaked it up like a sponge, I never wanted to forget this feeling. We sat on a bench at the corner of the dock and just talked as the sun went down. It was beautiful out. The sun dyed the ripples in the water, and occasionally a fish would break the surface, leaving a circle of orange water ripples that got larger and weaker as they traveled away from each other.

"I need a girl like you."

He had my attention.

"You understand me and make me happy. No one compares to you. It's hard to say it out loud but I do love you."

He hadn't ever told me he loved me until then. I had said it to him a week or so prior, but he hadn't replied. He'd stayed silent, and I'd smirked and then headed out of his apartment. It felt so good to finally hear him say it in words. I stood up, leaned over, grabbed his sun-kissed neck, and pulled him in for a long kiss. We locked eyes as I grabbed his hand and led him back into our room for the rest of the night.

It was these moments that I clung to and thought back to when he would say something to anger me and get under my skin. I would tell myself that it was only his inability to get close to someone or his cautious side that wasn't able to trust anyone enough to let me in. I believed he still loved me in the moments when he acted like he didn't and now he'd broken the barrier and was comfortable saying those words out loud to me. *I love you.* I would never get used to hearing that from him. I was determined to be there for him and be the one to show him how to let people in. I would build the foundation of our relationship one step at a time. *I could fix him.*

- - -

I sent him little notes to let him know he was on my mind, that he could trust me, and that I wanted no one else. It was true. No one piqued my interest the way he could. No one had a hold on me the way he did. I had had boyfriends before him. I had fallen for guys, but I was proud of my firm ground that I had always stood on. I knew my boundaries and didn't let a man cross them or even change my mind until Evan. He liked to know that he was in control. He needed the power trip. I let him persuade my thoughts in conversations, tell me what to wear, and even sway my opinions. My intention was to grow with him and to braid ourselves together as one, to blend him into me just as much as I blended parts of myself into him. Seeing a hard-headed—and I repeat, hard-headed—guy abandon his stubbornness to take my opinion over his own just to make me happy was way more powerful to me than any bouquet of flowers he could give me.

I know he cuddled me in the middle of the night when he thought I was sleeping. I know he could see himself with me for the long haul. He talked to me about sensitive, personal topics. He trusted me and confided in me, and as time went on, he truly let me in. The problem was that I always feared he would shut me out again, and when he did, it felt like we had to start all over again. Would I be telling my adult kids one day to chase after that love because I'd made the mistake of letting mine go, or would I look back and teach them the difference between lust and love based on my history with him? Could I pick a side to this guy so that this became a lesson, or would it be a twist of nonsense that I'd never figure out?

16

Rise Up

We spent Easter together. It was our first holiday together since neither of us went home to our families because we didn't have a lot of time off for Easter like we did for Christmas or New Year's. In addition, my family hadn't ever done much for Easter. I had a Christian background, so it was surprising that we never celebrated such a faith-focused holiday. Evan suggested we go to church and breakfast together. Dressed up in our expected pastel colors and mix of plaid and stripes, we headed over to the nearest church, which we should have just walked to judging by how far away we needed to park. It was standing room only, but it made sense, being a holiday and how fun the service was. The priest made jokes that made us all genuinely laugh, the music was beautifully played, and the people were bright and cheerful. We chose a chic bistro for breakfast, which at this point was actually brunch. The food was out-of-this-world delicious. I'm quite a food-motivated person, so I was on cloud nine. Also, it's said that your brain releases the same chemicals when you have good food as it does when you have sex. So, between the deliciously handsome man and the even more delicious food, I was certain that life didn't get better than this moment. I'm surprised we never went back to eat there again, come to think of it but Evan was probably avoiding an *I'll have what she's having* moment.

Kelsey invited us to her aunt's house because they were having a very large get-together and had a "more the merrier" mentality. I knew he would be welcome, but I still asked Kelsey if I could bring Evan since she made it clear didn't like him. She brushed it off and said, "of course he can come!" When we arrived, we were greeted with many hugs and kisses on the cheek by people we hadn't met before. They thought we were married and kept referring to Evan as my husband and me as his wife.

"Evan, I gave your drink to your wife." Kelsey's aunt said.

"Thank you so much." He never corrected her.

Could my heart literally explode? We were still full from eating brunch, so we only nibbled to be polite, but I wanted to go all in on those homemade cookies. They were mixed with peanut butter, butterscotch, and chocolate. Kelsey's family was very inviting, they wanted us to feel like family and not strangers. We made our way around the yard, talking to everyone and laughing so much. Evan still hadn't corrected anyone on their calling me his wife. It took Kelsey to hear it and say, "One day, Aunty, but right now, they're just dating."

I romanticized that a lot. "One day." It was heartwarming that Kelsey and her family saw us as a strong couple, despite her hate for him, and even more so that Evan wasn't turned off to the idea of being paired with me.

I was so happy to have a day like that that I still think back to it and smile. I really needed an easy, sunny day because a few days before I had been in the hospital for pain in my pelvic area after we had sex. It felt like I was being stabbed or like my uterus was going to fall out in one piece. I couldn't tell you which of the two of us was more concerned. Evan drove me to urgent care, but I went back with the nurse alone because I didn't know what to expect, and I didn't want Evan to witness anything too embarrassing. She took my vitals and asked me the standard questions, one of them being when my last period was. She asked if I had had sex in the past few weeks. I nodded and confirmed I had.

"Did you use protection?"

"No."

"Are you trying to get pregnant?"

"Absolutely not!"

"Hmmph. You know you're not being very smart then, right?"

Okay, rude. She gave me a pregnancy test, which was negative. She then told me that "candidly" she wouldn't believe that test for at least another week or so. She recommended I either come back in or take a home test because she didn't feel confident with the negative result. She finally got around to addressing the reason I came, the pain that was making every delayed second feel like a minute. Apparently, Evan had bruised my cervix. She then wanted to make sure that it was consensual sex and that I wasn't in an abusive relationship. After we talked, she felt a lot more confident that I was happy and just in a very heated, passionate relationship. She prescribed a pain reliever and abstinence for the next week.

I told Evan about the conversation I had had with the doctor, which he took very well. I told him not to worry about anything and that I wasn't worried a bit. Spoiler alert, the home test was negative as well. He really stepped up though for a guy who was focused on just having a good time and enjoying a year of no responsibility and drinking; now he was worried about an eight-pound load of responsibility and not running the opposite direction. I was so stress-free that week because I noticed that Evan was relaxed. He didn't seem stressed or concerned. I'm sure he was under the surface, but he never let it slip. It was the first time I had ever been told to worry about a situation like that. I didn't know what to expect or how to act, so I just told him we were fine and followed his lead. It made me fall more in love with him, knowing I could trust him to be there for me when it really mattered, theoretical or not.

There were many other times in the past when he would show up for me to prove he cared —like when he came over to my apartment even though he had a party going on at his. I didn't want to go to the party because I wanted a relaxing night in, and there were a few people going I didn't care much for.

"I'll see you at Evan's tonight!" a girl from class said to me on her way out.

"I'll see you next week," I replied.

Silence and a look of confusion were her reply. "Evan's party … tonight?" She tried again.

"No, I'm not going. I'm just not really in the mood for a party tonight. I want to stay in."

It was a hard sell because we all hung out together a lot, but I had hit my wall of being around him when we were "off." I couldn't stomach seeing him talk with other girls and wonder if maybe she would be staying over in my spot of the bed that night or if he would come and swoop me up in his arms with that infamous kiss on my neck and tell me he missed me. It was ruining me. The game and wonderment were off, and I didn't want the party; I just wanted him with me.

I was getting texts asking what time I was going to his place or asking if people were at my apartment pregaming and getting ready before we headed over. It was common to start the night at my place since it was right across the street from Evan's. I didn't reply to these texts for a while and played it off with an excuse, but to be honest, I was sad I was missing out on the fun that night, inside jokes, and side-crippling laughter. We had the best times every time we had a party, which was at least twice a week. I knew there were more to come and had to take a break for my own sanity.

Moments later, I had gotten a knock at my door. It was Evan. I broke into a smile and rolled my eyes as I opened the door in my pajamas. "Shouldn't you be at a party right now?" I asked as he walked in.

"Not without you." He grabbed my remote and made himself comfortable on my couch. "Come here," he added.

"No, you have a house full of people. Go hang out with them," I said with a chuckle. I was so happy with his gesture, but I couldn't let him miss out on his party.

"If you don't go, I don't go. Isn't that how it's supposed to work?" he asked, slipping that beautiful smile in at the end to show off how proud he was of himself.

"Yes, I suppose you're right."

"So, come here and watch this with me." He raised the blanket to show me my portion of it.

We ignored our buzzing phones, made our own inside jokes that night, and washed down our junk food with the wine I had in my fridge. In our own world and ignoring the chaos going on around us, we were together and fitting just as perfectly as ever.

17

Don't Say Girlfriend

He asked me to go back to his hometown so that he could show me around. He wanted me to meet his family and see where he was planning to go back and work after we graduated. I was usually really great when meeting the parents. I was polite and could talk to anyone about anything. This trip was really nerve-racking for me though because not only was I obsessed with this guy and wanted them to like me, but we were going for the whole weekend. It's one thing to meet family at a dinner but another to stay there for the weekend. I would have to be *on* at all times.

"You'll have a good time. Just don't be weird."

Oh great, Ev. Way to take my level-seven nerves up to a

full ten out of ten. He frequently described me as weird. I'm sure to him, I was. I always marched to the beat of my own drum and colored a little bit outside of the lines.

- - -

I was exhausted from the busy week of school we just wrapped up when we left that Friday afternoon. He told me that I could nap in the truck during the drive and handed me his sweatshirt. "Roll it up and use it as a pillow. Do you want me to turn the air down? I know you can't sleep if it's too cold."

"No, I'm okay, thank you." But what I meant was *No, don't do anything else for me. If I love you any more, I'll burst before I even get to meet your family.*

Before him, it took a lot for a guy to flatter or impress me. Like that iconic Shania Twain song, I wasn't impressed by much. So, me swooning over a guy suggesting I rest, handing me a sweatshirt (that he probably hadn't washed that month—a solid assumption based on his truck and his room), and modifying air temperature was very unlike me. Any other guy who had done the same thing in the past had gotten a simple thank-you. It was clues like this that nudged me to notice that there was something different going on with Evan. I extended his passenger seat all the way back, kicked off my shoes, and put my feet on the dash and his sweatshirt behind my head. I got to that perfect state of relaxation that happens right before you fall asleep when I heard a triple beep squeal from his radar detector hanging from his windshield followed by "Shhh, come on," in a soft whisper tone, followed by an accusing "You're going to wake her up" as he then pushed a sequence of buttons to make the beeping stop on my behalf. I didn't sleep after that. I laid there with my eyes closed, listening to him whisper-sing to the radio. I peeked through my eyelids just enough to see him bob his head to the same beat he tapped his fingers to on his steering wheel, just as gently as he was singing. He only sang along to the radio when he was in a great mood.

Even though I was going back to his hometown for the weekend to see where he grew up, wake up early to make breakfast with his mom, and help his dad with the funeral home, we weren't officially dating. He didn't refer to me as his girlfriend, just his friend Nellie or Nel. I had learned by this point that if I were to inquire about the status of our relationship or slip and call him my boyfriend, we would jump ten steps back to waiting ten minutes to get a text back because I waited eight minutes to text him back phase. I wouldn't dare jeopardize what I had.

- - -

I instantly loved his mom. His dad was great too when I got to meet him. He was out on a meeting when we arrived. She gave me a big hug the moment I walked through the door. "It's so nice to finally get to meet you, sweetie! I've heard just about everything there is to know about you."

"Oh, is that so?" I said with a smirk Evan's way.

"I don't talk about her that much, Mom. You're making it seem—" Evan was cut off by his overly accommodating mom grabbing our bags and telling us to leave our shoes on the small mat by the door.

"I love this mat, with sunflowers on it. They're my favorite flower," I said.

She had sunflower accents all throughout the house, in a very tasteful way. "Evan's grandmother, my mother, got me interested in them. She always had them in her house. In fact, some of these things are hers that I got after she passed."

"I'm so sorry to hear that she passed. My grandma is who got me interested in sunflowers too. She loves them as much as you do."

We continued to talk about everything under the sun. She asked where I grew up, how the drive was, how school had been going, and what I did beforehand, and time flew without me even realizing it.

His mom and I got along so well that I think he was afraid we were going to team up on him and change my last name that weekend. She was sarcastic and funny. She wanted to show me all around the house and tell me stories about her family and Evan as a kid. She had to have said fifty times how cute I was in the first day we were there. Needless to say, I was Mama Ellis-approved. Evan was close with his mom, so it was important to me that I got along with her. I didn't expect it to be so easy. They had sweet sayings and funny inside jokes that they brought up. They had a great relationship, his family. I wanted to be a part of that circle. I felt a genuine connection to them.

I felt like I was exactly where I should be. Like my path of life had led me to that family, that weekend, and that guy. Our red strings had pulled us together.

Michelle, his mom, and I didn't stop talking the whole time I was there. I wasn't that surprised that we got along so well. Guys who are close to their mothers are said to pick women who are similar. I think Evan did just that. She and I were both easygoing and very accepting of their work schedule. It was also my work schedule, so I understood when Evan pulled me aside to say, "I'm sorry, babe, but I have to help my dad for a little bit so that he can eventually come up for dinner. You can hang out up here with Mom though. Do you mind?"

"You know I don't mind a bit. Let me know if you need me to help, but otherwise, I'm happy to hang out with my new best friend."

He gave me a big and a perfect smile followed by a long kiss on my forehead.

Michelle and I began cooking dinner for the guys together. She did most of the leading, and I was more of her sous-chef. She pulled out her nice set of silverware and plates and asked me to set the table.

"Am I worth the special-occasion china?" I asked her jokingly.

"It's rare that Evan lets us meet his girlfriend, and it's even rarer that I actually like her, so yes, indeed," she answered excitedly.

"That means a lot. I really like you guys too. I'm having a great time here." I debated telling her that if Evan heard her use the word *girlfriend* that he would surely Kool-Aid Man himself through the wall, but I felt it was better saved for day two.

18

Say Something

Because of placement percentages, the school made a point to ensure we all got placed for careers as graduation was getting closer. I told our placement coordinator, Joni, that I would go anywhere. I wanted to move and spread my wings but didn't know where I wanted to go, so I was going to let her decide for me. Days later, she and I had a meeting about my options. She had picked up on my and Evan's relationship and told me that she had a job for me right by where he would be working. They were only twenty minutes apart. We were set up perfectly to actually start our relationship and grow together after college.

He and I had started talking about what our plan would

be after school and how we would stay together. This seemed to be the perfect solution. When he brought it up weeks prior, we were actually on one of our many breaks. I had come over to borrow a few of his movies, since I didn't have cable. I started doing that regularly since it was a four second walk over to his place. He was giving himself a haircut, shirtless, in his bathroom and popped his head out to tell me that he looked at a few places in the area for us to work at. He made the point that it was the midway point from where he grew up to where I had grown up. I think he was trying to prove that he could be considerate, which was exactly what we were arguing about this time around.

Letting fate decide my next step worked pretty well in my favor, so much so that I would have called it perfect and said that it was too good to be true. I mean, a job close to his with a great offer as well, too good! Cue Evan's inability to let me in. Joni told me she needed an answer in two days since someone else was also interested in the position. I went to talk with Evan about whether or not I would take the placement. It was still a bad time because we were a little uneasy with each other from our argument the week before. However, since we had the conversation many times about starting our life together and I had the perfect solution, I wasn't going to let that go to waste on a temporary argument. He came over so we could talk. I made him a drink and told him about the conversation I had had earlier that day with Joni. He didn't seem to have much to say other than he decided to officially accept the job with his family's firm back in his hometown. That was exactly the first part of what I wanted to hear, but he never said the second part. He never said he wanted me to move there and accept the job. I wasn't going to move hours away from where I currently

lived to be his almost neighbor if he didn't want me to be. There was an invitation that was very much required in that situation. "Do you want me to take the job near you then?"

He didn't say anything. He didn't say no, and he didn't say yes. Our eyes were locked in and his face was expressionless. I could feel my body temperature rising. Why wasn't he answering? I was getting really worried, and I'm sure my face was showing it.

"This is perfect for us, don't you think?" There was silence. "Will you say something?"

He looked down at his glass with a sad but stern expression.

"Evan?"

Still without saying a word, he stared right into my eyes as he moved to the edge of the couch like he was getting up.

"Don't get up. I'm not done talking to you." I was just pissed at this point, the kind of mad where the tears come even though you aren't actually crying. He got up from my couch, put his glass on the table, and just walked out. He left. To him, I didn't deserve an answer or a response of any extent. I wasn't even worthy of a breakup. At least lie to me or tell me that you have to think about it. Everything I put up with in the last year was all for that moment? There was no way that I was left to cry on my couch as he walked out. I heard my door shut. I sat there in that same spot with my elbows on my knees, my head resting in my hands. I felt hollow. Everything hurt, and yet everything was numb. I felt like I was going to be sick, but I didn't want to move. I was hurt by him but more so mad at myself for being so vulnerable to a guy who had yet to prove that he was worth all of this chaos. I just stared at nothing as tears fell.

I was worthless for days. Breakups are hard to begin with and even harder when you live across the street from him, sit next to him for eight hours a day, five days a week, and share the same friend group. I was madly in love with him and thought I had found my *one*. Part of me knew he didn't want us to end. I knew he'd change his mind. He did this. He'd flip and flop and take me with him on these emotional waves. But days later, we still hadn't talked, and that was not like us. We always caved in to each other, almost immediately.

A girl I was in class with noticed that something was off with me. She pulled me aside and asked me if she could give her honest opinion about Evan and me. I will never forget it. "I know this isn't my place and that it's totally different being in the relationship than on the outside, but you're better than this. I've overheard some of your conversations for a year now, and you honestly deserve so much better. Never settle please. For yourself, for all girls. You have more impact on the girls around you than you think you do."

It was what I needed to hear. She flipped a switch in me that shook me out of my gloom and told me I could do this. I could go on without him. I was ready to focus on me. I had been through hard times in life, and the previous lessons had prepared me for this moment. It was time to put myself first again and figure out what would make me happy. I just needed to heal first. I could finally see that sometimes you have to be done—not mad, not upset, just done. Against my will, I could hear Evan in my head saying, "I give it a week," in his smug tone.

19

Old News

I stayed home from classes one day because I was sick. It was just a cold or allergies, but when you mix that with stress, your body feels too weak to give the day any effort. I spent the day watching TV on the couch. I didn't move much and didn't plan to unless it was for hunger, which I eventually remedied when I just brought a bunch of snacks onto my coffee table, so they were more accessible for my lazy state. I was hours deep into my vegetative state when I got a call from Taylor. It was a loud, drunk phone call asking for a ride back to Evan's apartment. I was shocked because they didn't usually call me for drunken rides home, probably because most of the drinking happened at one of their apartments and because it was only the late afternoon to early evening time frame. How drunk could they be already?

"I know you're pretending to be sick so you can sit on your ass all day, but can you please come get us?"

"I'm actually sick, Taylor, and your screaming into the phone doesn't help with the headache."

He must have known he was losing my interest because he handed the phone to Evan and slurred a broken sentence to get him caught up on our phone call. Then I heard, "We're not far from you, and once you drop us off at my place, you're basically already home. Then you can go back to bed!"

He had a point, but it was a tough sell. We were on the biggest of our many breaks, and I didn't want to move from the couch or my eleventh sequential binge-watching episode that day, but nevertheless, I couldn't let him down. He needed something and asked *me*. Part of me knew that I was just being used, but I cared about him and Taylor and wanted to have my hero moment. I put myself together, which only consisted of a few strokes of mascara and a pair of leggings to match my messy bun and sweatshirt and then headed out to get them. I was told that I could honk the horn when I pulled in, and they would come down. I should have known better.

I ended up staying for an hour and left with a car full of people. The party continued on at Evan's place, and they begged me to come up for one drink. They swore that the vodka would dry up my sinuses and make me feel better. It was worth a shot. During my hour at the previous party, Ev said that he and this older lady who also went to school with us, one of the big partiers at the school, had a really good talk earlier that day and that he wanted to tell me about it. I had no patience, so I was incredibly restless but also knew I wasn't having the conversation that night with the number of empty bottles on the counter. Moments later, I heard parts of their continued conversation coming from the kitchen while I was throwing darts with Taylor, against my sick will, one room over.

I overheard, "Do you love her? … Then what are you afraid of?"

My heart was beating out of my chest because I knew this conversation was leaning in my favor and hoped that the conversation was about her convincing him to take it seriously this time around. I took my next turn in darts, and then I walked past the kitchen "nonchalantly" to use the restroom, thinking I would catch some more of the conversation, but instead, I saw them making out! Making out! What the fuck? I nearly tripped over myself. This old lady was crawling up my man like her wrinkle cream was on top of his head. I got so sick to my stomach. The cold I had was suddenly the most insignificant of my symptoms. The room went from totally still to spinning out of control. I was instantly overwhelmed and hot and needed to leave. I pretended I didn't see anything and made a casual excuse to leave. I cried from his door to mine and then got pissed and told myself that was the last straw and he was done. Yes, I have a bottomless collection of "last straws".

We're done. I'm getting over him once and for all.

20

Mr. Money

There were a few dates in between that piqued my interest during the time after breaking up with Evan, none of which could be red strings—of that, I was quite certain. I had actually sworn off dating. I said I was done with dating, but those past few months proved to me that I was pretty awful at keeping promises to myself. I realized I dropped a lot of promises to myself and realizing it and wanting to change it is the first step, but Rome wasn't built in a day. Two days after I swore off dating, Kelsey swore to me that this guy was a great fit for me, so much so that I would second-guess wanting to move. He was her boyfriend's best friend, so it was destined to work out, right? Super wrong. He was handsome, he was interesting, and he had done very well for himself career wise and liked to flaunt his money. In fact, I don't think he knew what humble meant. But that wasn't my problem at the time. He was so fun to be around, a nice way to get my mind off Evan, maybe even make him a little bit jealous in the interim. He pampered me with nice dinners and lavish nights out downtown. He also got us tickets to the Blackhawks, which is of course my all-time favorite team. Evan had gotten me to the sixth row. I never thought anything would ever top it. Well, Mister Money got us tickets to a sold-out game in the third row. Let me repeat that—third-row seats to the Blackhawks. I was speechless. I don't even remember speaking after he told me, but I must have said yes because we were in the lobby of a very fancy hotel checking into our room. Yes, we got a room when we could have very easily just gone back to my apartment. Why be frugal when you can waste money? It was going very well even though it was very new. He was so extra with everything he did that moving fast in a relationship was his routine. We had a few drinks at the hotel bar and even more from the fridge in our suite. After all of the drinking and excitement got to my head, I changed into my newest Blackhawks jersey that I had bought just for this game. I was ready for it. We took a cab to the stadium and grabbed more drinks from concession along with some nachos. I got to the seat, nay, stumbled to the seat in the third row. I went to grab my phone to start taking a hundred photos when my jaw hit the sticky, cold arena floor. My drunk ass left my phone in the hotel room. I was living out one of my wildest dreams and had no way to document it. I thought to myself, *Nellie, sit back and watch the game, soak it up, and live in the moment,* but I knew my blood alcohol level wasn't going to let me remember anything. I don't remember much at all actually except for clips of it. I know I stole Mr. Money's phone to snap a few pictures and sent them to myself. I also know that he and I got separated at the end of the night when I went to brave the very busy ladies' room and he didn't stay put where I told him to.

I still missed Evan though. Mr. Money and I were just really good at being stupid and having fun together. We drank too much and spent too much money. It wasn't sustainable. We were both clearly just filling a void or living out some rebound experience to have fun and enjoy life while laughing and trying to forget the people we were really thinking about. I didn't see much harm in it until we went out to his old college town the next weekend. We got separated from each other again somehow, and I got lost while being a little drunk. I didn't even have my debit card to get a cab because I gave it to Mr. Money when he asked if he could use it to get $40 from the ATM. I thought it was out of character but didn't mind because he had bought enough for me at that point that I could certainly give the guy $40. Well, I was lost and roaming, and he was also drunk and somewhere so loud that I couldn't comprehend where exactly he was when I called him. So, what was the first thing I did when I hung up with him? Well, yes, I texted him for clarification of his location, and then while walking to that spot, called Evan. He teased me for a while. "Aren't you supposed to be out with your new loverboy?"

"Oh, I am," I said, making sure my eye roll was obvious through my voice.

"Miss me yet?"

"So much. Will you actually come here please and get me and take me home? I don't like him, and I really just want to be on the couch with you under my blanket watching our stupid shows instead of lost out here." I'm sure there were so many slurred words in that, but he got the point.

"Ha! You're so predictable, you know it? I'm very far from you though. Why aren't you with him? Where are you? Are you safe?"

"I have no idea—wait. I think I found where he is. Gotta go."

"I'm sure you'll be texting me soon."

I really did want to just be back at his apartment with him under the fleece blanket that I claimed as "my blanket." It was more oversized than any blanket needed to be, in the corner of his couch where both ends of the sectional pieces met. It was so comfortable there, and I was so out of my element here. Who were all of these people and—why the hell did my bank just text me to confirm at $450 withdrawal? Would this night ever end?

- - -

Mr. Money withdrew $450 from my card and gambled it all away on those stupid electronic gaming machines by the time I found him in his stupid college town. Needless to say, that was the last time I saw him. Let's chalk that up as a loss for Kelsey's attempt at being cupid.

21

I'd Rather Be Poor

I practically ran back to Evan after Kelsey's lover fail. When I made it back home, I first needed a day of me-time to recover from the crazy weekend, but then the next day, I went over to Ev's to hang out after class. Being neighbors made it so easy to spend time together, whether it was to borrow something or have some company on a quiet night or even in the dead of winter when there was a travel advisory. We had a few of those, but it wasn't anything that couldn't be fixed by a pair of snow boots and his bulk-sized supply of hot chocolate. We had days of uninterrupted time together—no class, no work, no other visitors. He was a great neighbor.

I brought over snacks in my sweatpants and messy hair. I picked a movie that I was excited to watch. I had been wanting to see it for a while, but I should have known better. A few minutes later, I was so comfortable on the couch, lounged out under what I claimed as my blanket, enjoying my drinks and snacks and zoned into the movie. Evan, however, was zoned in on me and tapped the arm of his recliner, so I shook my head and returned the gesture with a tap on the couch beside me. This went on a few times mixed in with some laughs and eye rolls. I finally broke the silence with "I'm pretty sure this was on a movie."

"Will you just come lay with me?"

"In the recliner? Wouldn't the couch make more sense?"

All I got in return were sad puppy eyes.

I dragged my blanket across the floor with me as I headed over to sit with him on his beloved chair. It wasn't possible to both sit in the chair without spooning, so once again, he got his way and a bonus cuddle. Time went on, and I noticed he was leaning his head on mine and playing with my hair. It was the subtleties with him that made me melt. They were rare but genuine, so like a bee to pollen, I soaked it up. He pulled me in, which I didn't think needed to happen when there were two people under a giant blanket on a one-person chair. He made sure there wasn't any air between our bodies. My body being curled into his was his kryptonite. He had said to me previously before a time or two that he loved my body just being near his and that in those moments, just a touch would arouse him. I never fully understood until this night. As we were lying there on the chair, he started to breathe heavier and kiss my neck, which was my weakness. He whispered in my ear to let me know he was turned on, but I wasn't going to give in to having sex with him, and as it turned out, I didn't have to. I had completely tuned out the movie at this point and was fully immersed in him. With my eyes closed, I could tell he was getting more and more into it until his neck kisses stopped, and I could feel his head buried into mine and his body go weak. Did he just get off by kissing me? He did! Need I mention the ego boost of arousing him without even trying to? This guy never ceased to amaze me.

"You're incredibly sexy," he said as he got up off the chair.

I smiled as I realized he was crazy because my hair was wrecked, and my outfit was anything but flattering. I was in an oversized college sweatshirt and my sweatpants that I should have thrown away years ago, but that's the recipe for great sweats.

22

Spades

As much as I wanted to be anywhere that he was, life still wasn't easy with Evan. We couldn't mesh back together as well as we had hoped to. Tensions remained high, and it seemed more off and on than steady. This was mainly because we were both "flight" in the fight-or-flight response style. We had our guard up at the first sign of a disagreement. We were not good at working arguments out in the moment. I needed time to brew on my response for a while longer if I wanted it to come off as reasonable or convincing. Any thoughts I had in the moment were brash and what I believe to be out of character because he could make my blood boil with a single word. He needed space, to be in control of his environment at all times, especially in an argument. He would walk away until he was confident with a response or solution. So basically, any disagreement would shatter us momentarily.

We had our intimate nights together quite often, whether we were dating or hating each other, and whether at his place or my place, they were full of heated hate-sex and loving cuddling afterward. Talk about a confusing combination. I didn't know how to feel, either in the moment or afterward. Keeping track of all these emotions was a full-time job. He knew when I was angry with him, but he also knew how to dissolve my anger completely. Although it's great when your partner can ease your anger and change your mood, there is a downside when it comes to setting boundaries and trying to get your point across.

Along with trying to get my point across, I also tried to get over this guy and move on. I wanted to be able to be interested in other guys. I blame myself and my occasional lack of charm for this next failed attempt. I was at nice dinner with a very handsome, had-a-successful-job-in-a-skyscraper looking guy and while talking and filling any silence between us, the waiter came over to take our order. Unfortunately, one of the many "past times" of small-town folk is intentionally mispronouncing words and finding it comical, therefore doing it frequently. So much so, that it becomes habit. I forgot to turn on my sophisticated brain and accidentally ordered "saLmon" for dinner, it just slipped out and I was immediately embarrassed. The look of dissatisfaction on this unsuspecting guy's face told me that this would be the last time he took me on a date and that I better eat my "saLmon" quickly. I made sure to more thoroughly think before I spoke as to not dig myself into a deeper hole. I didn't belong in his world and he made that pretty clear as our food came. Oh well, at least I tried.

I ran right back to my comfort zone, yet again. I reverted back to Evan and to making Kelsey roll her eyes, but Evan *got* me. I've been told that when you find the male version of yourself is when you find your soulmate. Well, I found the male version of myself, and we bickered, we drove each other crazy, and we went from love to hate and back to love as quickly as the changing of tone in our voices, so we'll go ahead and call that one a myth. I had a tendency to run at the first sign of confrontation or if someone got too close in a way that I wasn't familiar with. It was easier to say goodbye and walk away than it was to talk through what happened and clarify our feelings until our anger was resolved. When you get two people like that in a relationship, well, it turns into the kind of relationship your friends hate.

A few times during our breaks, he had another girl stay over. He assured me they didn't have sex, but I never believed him. He was hot, and I wasn't the only one who saw it. Girls flirted with him regularly and stared at him longer than I was comfortable with. I had enough of the breaks in our relationship and just wanted to be together steadily. I was over the games and was finally set on choosing fight over flight. No more running away. I told him firmly in that moment that I was putting my foot down. He wore a shit-eating grin when I yelled at him saying that no one was ever to be in my spot again and that I didn't care if it was the queen, a homeless dog, or a celebrity. That was my spot. "Got it?" I demanded. He kept the shit-eating grin on his face as he grabbed me by the front waistband of my jeans and pulled me in for a kiss.

"Then don't fuck it up, and I won't let other girls in my bed," he replied.

Oh did my blood begin to boil. The flight mode made

me pull back and head toward the door, but the fight mode's alarm was blasting. Come on! *Me* not fuck it up? I couldn't let him get away with that. After all, I was the one at his beck and call, I was the one who let him get away with everything, and I was the one who was always right there waiting for him to run back. He was the one who kept pulling away and messing up. If smoke could actually come out of ears, I could have peeled the hideous wallpaper border in his 1995-styled bedroom. "Have. You. Lost. Your. Damn. Mind? *Me* not fuck it up? Really, Ev?"

"Don't be so short tempered. Take a joke."

"I can take a joke. That was you being an asshole and calling it a joke," I clarified. "You need to find the fine line."

"Okay, okay. I'm sorry I made a bad joke. You want to be serious, and I get it. I'm here, aren't I?"

Our relationship was so frequently flipping from love to hate that it was exhausting, mentally and physically. I could joke about the repetitive makeup sex also wearing me out, but it didn't feel funny anymore. I was wearing thin on this roller coaster of emotion, and it started to feel like mental abuse. It was amazing to love him when it was good but being with him had very negative consequences on my mental health. If I could be certain that he and I would work out, then maybe it would be worth it to put up with the chaos. Unfortunately, he was so unpredictable that I had no idea what each day would bring. When I woke up next to him, would I get a loving kiss on the shoulder, a back rub, or the boot? Loving someone so hard and not getting equal love back is a level of pain that you don't forget. But the old saying of what doesn't kill you makes you stronger isn't just a cliché. Emotional pain really builds you up on the inside, and as soon as you can step back to see what you're dealing with and decide to make a plan to change it, you're in for a treat.

He and I were up late playing cards in my apartment, and I could tell the connection wasn't there. He kept checking his phone and texting that annoying vibration back. He put an ace on the table and then immediately went to his phone and told me to call it as he looked down, texting, "High or low? Up to you."

That was it.

That stupid card.

That was the end of it all. He just wanted me to decide the value of the card, but a rush of metaphor flooded my head. Our relationship turned me into that deck of cards. He could take pieces of me so tiny one day at a time that I didn't notice myself going from fifty-two cards to fifty-one, tearing me down from fifty-one to fifty, and changing me slowly until there was only one card left in my pile. The ace. And it was up to me to decide my value. Lowest value or the highest?

It was as if my chest opened up, and I got my first breath of peaceful air.

I must have been blankly staring out into the distance as I played the metaphor through my mind more and more deeply.

"Nellie, hello? Pick."

I stared at him blankly. "Can I pick bedtime? I'm really tired and have an early morning. You can go."

He was stunned. It was the first time all night that his phone buzzed, and he didn't reach for it immediately. "Uh-huh, okay. Sure." He got up to leave and stopped right beside me. "Kiss?"

"No, thank you. Good night."

23

Go For It

I reached out to a few funeral homes in different areas but wasn't getting excited about any of them. I looked in all areas of New York, upstate, downstate, centerstate, if that's a thing, but nothing sparked excitement like Benton's Funeral Home. I reached out to them to apply for an intern position, but they told me they had just recently filled it. My heart sank because not only is rejection hard, but it really was the only funeral home I had been wanting to work at. I only knew what I had read about it from researching it, but it had a certain charm and apparent level of excellence that I really wanted to be a part of. Days had passed. I was exhausted through and through and needed a win. I was sitting in Evan's living room with Taylor and Kelsey and Evan's latest flirt that he swore was just a friend when my phone rang. I didn't have the number saved, but the city listed below the number was New York, and there was only one place in New York that would be calling me. I quickly got up and went out the front door so that I could hear the call clearly and without any talking in the background.

It was them! It was Benton's asking me to do a phone interview the following week. They explained that because of the college I was attending and it's high merit, they couldn't pass up having me on their team so they were willing to add a position for me. I went from feeling like I was in a gray cloud to seeing the light at the end of the tunnel. Everyone must have been able to see the excitement on my face when I walked back in because they all stopped talking to ask who was on the phone. I beamed as I told them and didn't let the look on Evan's face sway my mood. I had so much to look forward to now, including graduation, which was weeks around the corner.

I had zoned in the last few weeks of classes and studied from the time I left classes until it was dark out and I was the last one in the coffee shop. A lady watched me as I moved my frappe away from my national board exam study guide and thoroughly checked to make sure the table was clean before I set the book back down, as I set my condensation-soaked cup on my MacBook laptop. I felt her judging me and my choices to protect the book over the laptop—$100 versus $1,000 was a clear difference in value, but what this stranger didn't know was that this book held every bit of information that I needed to know for my board exam. It made perfect sense to me, or I had just studied too hard and lost my common sense. Graduation was coming up and so were a long list of vital exams. I needed to push through with my last bit of sanity I had. No distractions, just hard work and a degree to prove it.

24

Moving On

I had gone out to New York once in the time between graduation and moving. That trip was just for one day to meet the staff and do a working interview. I felt so professional and accomplished getting on the airplane in a suit to head to New York for my interview for my new profession. It was a new version of me, grown-up me. I'd always seen businesspeople on planes with their briefcases and tablets making phone calls and appearing to be succeeding in life. I was finally fitting into that atmosphere. This was what I had envisioned and hoped for.

I was euphoric after the working interview because it went perfectly. I had my offer letter in hand and read it while eating dinner at the airport waiting for my flight. It was a decent offer; I could afford the rent on the apartment I wanted, and I would be able to save along the way. My apartment was a huge deal for me. I value my alone time and my personal space, so having that ideal place to call home meant everything to me, especially after the chaotic year I had just had and the emotional toll this career path put on me. I needed to know that I was in control of where I would be calling *home*.

I instantly connected with the staff at Benton's. They were side-cramping hilarious. They had so much personality and were not at all what I expected, in the best way. I was familiar with the field and the people who usually worked in it. Funeral directors are always prim, proper, and reserved, but this place had a completely different feel than I was used to. They truly enjoyed their work and working together. They came off as a real family right away. I knew instantly that I would be honored to work with them. Not for nothing, the funeral home was beautiful! Straight out of a magazine. It felt more like walking into a hotel lobby than it did a funeral home. Watching all of these positive features unfold in front of me, I was elated. I was so proud of myself for taking this jump and heading into this next chapter of life so courageously.

Another thing that made this company stand out was that they had multiple locations. Each was run by a different manager, per the funeral direction operations law, but they all worked together closely as a team. My first week on the job, they wanted me to work a day at each of the locations to familiarize myself with the procedures and layouts of each. It was toward the end of my first week there, and I was working at their second biggest location with the manager. We were going over where they kept things in that facility while doing some busy work and small talking. The location manager and

I were both pretty open people so conversation was flowing well, and I had talked with him previously during my training process so it was a familiar conversation. He said I had to meet his nephew because after getting to know me throughout this week, we seemed to have so much in common. He was really pushing the introduction and said that he was quite confident that we would make the perfect couple, or at least be best friends. I was in a strange city without knowing anyone within hundreds of miles except the new faces I had met that week, and I'd been taught not to shit where I ate, so dating my new boss's nephew sounded like a very messy situation that I wanted no part in. Not to mention the emotional scarring that I was still trying to heal from. I didn't want to offend him though by turning down his idea so quickly, an idea that he seemed quite proud that he had, so I chuckled and thanked him for the compliment. I explained that I wasn't interested in being set up in that moment and that I was still focusing on getting into the swing of my new routine.

"Let me know if you change your mind." He dropped it.

I continued to keep my head down, work hard, and repeat. The days were so long, and the new information was flooding in so heavy that in the evenings when I would get home, I fell asleep almost immediately on the couch before even making dinner. I woke up in the middle of the night multiple times on the couch with the TV and lights still on because I had dozed off unexpectedly. As time went on, I got more used to my routine, and the information wasn't as new, so it was easier for my brain to process it. I slowly became more human again. I became friends with my coworkers and got to hang out with them outside of work a few times to girl-talk and chat about life in general. This was a moderately rare occasion though only because we had different schedules.

When they were working, I would spend my evenings out at baseball games. I visited all the local landmarks on my days off and learned a lot about my new home little by little. I was loving it. It was a beautiful city, and I was seeing parts of it that locals hadn't even visited. I was great at my job and really proud of myself but was also beginning to feel pretty lonely. I got my fill of talking to people at work, but I still wanted and needed friends. I was craving camaraderie with more people than the two girls I worked with.

My neighbor was cute. We'd cross paths outside a few times and make small talk. He asked me on a date, and because his license plate had a Purple Heart emblem on it, I knew his odds of being a serial killer were low so I let him take me to dinner and show me around his favorite places of the city, one of which was an underground tunnel that, despite the Purple Heart emblem, I was certain was the spot where I'd be killed. *See you soon, Jesus. Thanks for a good run, God.* I mean, come on, who would assume that taking a girl to an abandoned tunnel covered in graffiti and what I'm hoping wasn't blood would be a great first date? But he was amiable, and conversation flowed easily, so I enjoyed myself again when my blood pressure got back to normal. Something about his personality was too strong for me though. He wasn't a loud person. In fact, he was reserved, but he was so large with his words and overpromised on everything that I could tell it wasn't a good match. He came off too strong, and it turned me away. On our first date, he talked about wanting to take me to Germany and said that he had always wanted to take a private jet to Mexico just for lunch. This was some girl's wildest dream, and I'm sure he's found the girl for him, but it wasn't me. I know he meant well, but why waste his time or mine? I would try to time my trips outside around his so that I wouldn't have to have the awkward "It's not you; it's me" conversation. Though out of respect for this very kind veteran, I had to have it anyway when he brought flowers to my door and apologized for scaring me off.

I also thought the security guard of the hospital I frequented for work was really cute. I tried to stalk him on social media a few times by the name on his badge. He was tall, dark, and handsome and wore a uniform to work. Yes, please. He ended up finding me on social media one day, and I thought, *Okay, he's interested in me as well. Maybe we'll go on a date.* It actually came off as a squeal and a shimmy, but that was what I was thinking anyway. I immediately told the girls at work, and we started creeping on all of his pictures together. The girls and I referred to him as "boyfriend" but never to his face of course. Any time we had to work with this hospital, they sent me there in hopes that he would be on duty. He of course never knew why it was always me who showed up on the calls all of a sudden, and I never told him. One day, he made my upper lip curl when he came trotting around the corner with two nurses who were actively drooling over him. He carried himself in such a cocky and conceited way around them, which was a side of him I hadn't ever seen before. He continued to blatantly flirt with the two of them back and forth, and they were eating it up. He then thought that looking up at me to include me in this ego game would be a success, but it created a screeching halt in my interest altogether. My imaginary boyfriend was a major tool in real life. *Next.*

Although I am a very social person and love having a circle around me, I love staying at home and hanging out with myself just as much. But after a few months of being in this new place and not being able to meet friends organically, because my life revolved around work or going out to places by myself (which I had thought would be the best way to meet friends but wasn't as realistic as I had thought), I was starting to get lonely. I missed my friends back home and was in need of some socialization that didn't revolve around work. Mind you, this whole time, my boss was still subtly hinting at his nephew being a perfect match for me. So I thought, *What the heck? I don't have to date him, but I can be his friend.* I told him I would take him up on his "best friend" offer in his nephew and asked him what his nephew's name and number were. I sent him a text simply saying hello and how I got his information. He replied hours later, knowing who I was already, with an invitation to a baseball game with him and his friends. I had the night off, loved the local team, and replied with a yes.

I wasn't ready to be in a relationship yet, but I was ready for some friends my age in this foreign town. You can only go to so many baseball games by yourself before you start to feel like a team stalker (and no, none of the players were cute; I checked). So I went against everything I was taught as a kid and decided I would drive to this stranger's house, knock on his door, and voluntarily walk into it.

He bought the house just a month or so before we met. His uncle had been keeping me in the loop on all of his latest achievements in a way I could only assume was to attract me to him. He showed me pictures of the house on his phone and a few of his nephew, Jordan, cooking dinner on his first-owned oven. Jordan was cute, and the house was cute too. It wasn't my style, but in a light-spirited moment, I decided to play along with his uncle's pride and joke that that window there was the window to my room and the circle window over there was my bathroom and made a few other mentions of it being my future home. I had never even met this guy, and that may as well have been the window to the hall closet for all I knew or cared.

As I was getting closer to his house to meet him and one of his friends before we went to the baseball game, I was getting a little nervous, but not overly so because I was pretty outgoing, an introverted extrovert to be exact. I was most nervous about where to park. Did I knock or ring the doorbell or both? Should I offer to drive so that I didn't get in a car with these guys? Not that I thought they would abduct me, but I didn't want to get stuck in a situation I was uncomfortable with and have to rely on someone else to get me home. I recognized the house from the picture his uncle had showed me, so I knew I was at the right one. I made sure to park on the street, just the right amount of on the grass to be out of the road but not too much that I was rude for driving on this guy's new lawn. I got out, made sure I had my purse, locked my door, and headed up to his. The guy who came to the door was far more handsome than I had expected from his pictures. Granted, they were from either five years ago or a poorly taken phone pic, so I didn't have much to go on. He opened the door with a beaming smile and a friendly "Hi, I'm Jordan. Come on in!"

My eyes took a mental picture of that bright, sparkling smile on the tall, dark, and handsome man leaning forward to hold the door open for me. I thought to myself, *Oh crap*. I didn't want to think he was cute. I wanted a friend only. I pushed the crush down deeper and took a quick glance around the house from his living room before we headed out to the game together.

One of his good friends was already there and also very personable. They were easy to talk to and made me feel really comfortable. We had plenty to discuss on our ride downtown to the game and shared a few good laughs. It was so refreshing to be in healthy, positive company with people my age who loved their lives and enjoyed the little things. All of the friends we met up with at the stadium welcomed me into the group like I had known them for a while, which was so unexpected since I hadn't ever even heard any of these people's names before and didn't even know the two people I drove there with. I got along with one friend of his more so than the others, Kate. She was the one who got us the tickets for free through her work, so I made sure to thank her for allowing me to mooch off of her work benefits. As we got talking, we came across a lot of things we had in common, and we spent most of the game just chatting and talking about how I landed in New York and what she was doing in school and with work at that time. I had no idea at the time but later found out that Kate wasn't always so welcoming to new people in the friend group, that she could usually be described as the bitchy friend who wasn't usually a fan of other girls. Maybe it was because I too wasn't usually a fan of other girls (rooted in my many years growing up with them making fun of me in junior high and high school), but Jordan said that his friends were all talking about how I was an honorary member of the group because I passed the Kate test. I was happy that I said yes to hanging out with Jordan and even happier that I felt like I was finally making friends in this foreign place. He seemed like such a good guy, and I was seeing this more and more throughout the night. He was well-mannered but snarky. I didn't let my crush grow though. I made sure to bottle it down. I was just grateful for everything I was experiencing in that moment. I made sure not to focus on him too much also. I didn't want his friend group to associate us together.

25

Taylor, Go To Bed

My group of college friends and I had gotten together to spend the weekend on the lake a few times during school and it was time for another weekend together. This time, it was to catch up on what we've been up to because it had been a while since graduation. The planning of it went as usual. We stayed at the same spot, with the same people and planned to do the same things: water sports, a drive-in movie, and late-night campfires. We didn't change much except for the fact that Evan and I were no longer a couple or actively trying to be. Yet, our friends didn't believe that we were apart. As much as they hated us being together, they also loved pushing us closer to each other. They were just as messed up in our relationship as we were apparently. Truthfully, I was really nervous about seeing Evan again after being apart for the longest amount of time since we had met. School was over, I was starting my routine in New York, and he was finding his new routine of working with his family and putting that degree to use.

As we arrived one by one, it felt like nothing had changed. We all picked up right where we left off. There weren't any awkward silences or need for ice breakers, and better yet, no one changed a bit since school. It took me right back to how it was during that year together. It was hard to go from seeing these friends every single day to being apart for months. I knew it would be even harder to say goodbye to them all, all over again when this extended weekend was over.

We were back; the group was together again and rowdy as usual. I was continually on-guard, ready for Evan to pull something or say something that would send us spiraling again. I was certainly overthinking everything he did, like *Did he put our song on the speaker intentionally, or was it on shuffle? Did he mean to stare at me just then, or was he spacing out?*

The first day on the water had come to an end as the sun went down, so we all headed in to change into something warmer, grab some campfire ingredients, and head out to the fire for hotdogs, s'mores, and a cooler of our favorite drinks. Evan and I shared a case of Corona Light, with extra limes. That was our latest go-to. It changed from vodka and water to light beer; throwing up wasn't as fun of an outcome anymore. We reminisced on the past times we shared at the lake and how we promised to come back at least once a year to stay in touch. There was a constant crossfire of conversations going over one another—stories of what we were up to since graduation, things we hated about the work field, and things we loved about it.

I headed inside to "break the seal" and re-up on the chocolate bars. Unsurprisingly, when I left the bathroom, there was a certain tall, attractive temptation standing in front of me. He became more delightful to look at the more I drank, but I promised myself that I wouldn't melt into him again. I tried to break the tension-filled silence with small talk, but he shut it down without courtesy. "I miss you. You look good."

Oy vey.

Nel, breathe. Stop.

"Thank you" was all I was able to force out as I squirmed past him in the doorway.

"I give that act of resistance one more beer, and then you're mine," he said with a disgusting amount of grace.

"Oh, there's a lot of confidence spewing from those lips, sir. What makes you think that?"

"Because it's us, and there's no stopping it."

Touché.

In an effort to disagree, I smirked and rolled my eyes. He was right. That was us. There was no stopping it. But there was a word in both of those sentences, one that I was going to hold true to: *was*—not *is*, not *will be*—*was*.

Hours passed, beers were drunk, s'mores were eaten, and stories were shared. Slowly, friends tapped out and went inside for bed until there were only three of us still awake and going strong. It seemed to always be Evan, Taylor, and me at the end of the night. Taylor was about four sips of beer away from his eyes closing involuntarily in his lawn chair. Evan and I would exchange glances and chuckle every two seconds at Taylor's drunken expense until walking him inside was the mandatory next step.

"I'll handle the fire and food if you can take him in." Evan said as he grabbed a bottle of sand.

"No, let's … more. I … see ya'more," Taylor slurred.

"Sounds like a plan," I confirmed as I reached out for Taylor's hand. "Come on, bud."

A few chuckles and a sleeping Taylor later, it was Evan and I alone in the kitchen, talking over lamplight. We talked for a while longer as I sat on the island counter and he rummaged through the fridge for drunk snacks.

"Baaaabe," he cooed, "will you make me something?"

Puh-lease. What a ploy.

"Fine, but only because I'm hungry too."

I wasn't about to literally *make* anything to eat so he and I ate out of the family-sized serving bowl of pre-made salad we found in the fridge as we carried on our conversation completely oblivious to the time that passed or the lowering level of veggies left in the bowl.

Dunt. His fork hit the bottom of the glass serving bowl.

I curled forward in laughter. "Ev! We ate the whole thing!" Minutes of laughter passed as I took the dish to the dishwasher to hide the evidence. Not only was that salad intended for the entire group's lunch tomorrow, but if they knew Evan and I had stayed up until four in the morning, just the two of us, they would never let the poking and the jokes end. They loved to bring up our relationship in a playful, joking tone that neither of us were too fond of. It meant more to us than a good punch line for a joke. As I closed the dishwasher door, I felt his arms wrap around me, and he kissed the back of my head.

"I really miss this."

"Me cleaning up after you? I don't." I said as I turned around towards him.

He chuckled. "No, Nel. You and me and—" He leaned in for a kiss.

"No, Evan, I really can't."

"Why not? Did you all of a sudden stop loving me?"

"Well, uh, I—"

He beelined right for a kiss on my neck, and his leg slid in between mine as he picked me up onto the island counter.

"Stop," I said as I pushed him away. "I can't do this anymore. I'm really happy with my life now." That last sentence stuck with me. Why did I say it that way? Was I mentally happy with the idea of being free from his mind games, or was I physically happy and not needing to feel his touch of "approval" anymore? It wasn't that I didn't enjoy it anymore, because I certainly did. I think my body went on autopilot to push him away because my heart and head both wanted him to continue. I knew where it'd lead, and I knew I'd love it. So did he.

He hung his head low and said, "All right. I'll see you in the morning," as he rubbed my cheek with his thumb. He kissed my forehead and turned the lamp off. I didn't leave my spot on the island for a bit afterward, I was just trying to replay it all in my head to figure out what the hell had just happened.

I woke up feeling like a freight train had hit me, but that was the normal aftermath when hanging with these guys, especially on vacation. We brewed coffee and all sat around the living room together competitively comparing who was more hungover and who felt the worst. It didn't take long before we moved on from our hangovers and were in our swimwear and heading down to the water to do it all over again. I grabbed the sunscreen and towels, and the guys grabbed the drinks and snacks. It was our own form of paradise under the sun, on the boat, laughing at the unexpected backflips people did as they flew off the inner tubes at high speed. Just as true friends do, we were able to reconnect and not skip a beat after time apart. I was still the butt of everyone's jokes and took the blame for anything from the clouds covering the sun to them forgetting to bring down the Bluetooth speaker, etc. All of which I rarely had anything to do with. But I didn't mind. I was so happy to be on vacation and so used to them razzing me about every little thing that I just rolled my eyes and continued enjoying the day. Evan acted like the night before never happened. He was a pro at that. None of our friends knew anything about it either, until lunchtime came.

Justin asked, "Where the hell is the salad? I swear it was in here."

Evan shot a glance at me with a guilty-as-hell grin, and I couldn't help but laugh.

"Did you guys take it out to the fridge in the garage?" Justin asked accusingly.

"No, I didn't see a salad," Evan lied.

I stayed silent because if I opened my mouth to say anything, they'd see right through it and I knew better than to admit anything around these guys. It was clear as day that Justin didn't believe a word that we said to him, but he dropped it and our late-night salad-binge-eating session remained a moderate secret. A good sunburn later and we were in our usual nightly routine of Evan and me being the last ones awake. I think it's because he and I could talk for hours about anything or because a few minutes prior, he convinced Taylor that it was time for him to go to bed again.

We got gawked at when we communicated around our friends, so late nights were our only peaceful times alone. I'd be lying if I said I didn't look forward to that part of the night. He was my person in that group, the one I looked forward to seeing and catching up with most. He felt the same way. He walked down to my bedroom and stood in my doorway with a popsicle like it was a peace offering for scaring the crap out of me when I turned around to a tall, drunk man standing in my dark doorway. We sat on the couch outside my room and talked for an hour or so about our friends and our impression of how they were all doing after graduation based on the stories we had heard as we all caught up throughout the day. Then we got on the taboo subject of his dating life and the failed relationship he tried to start with a girl—a relationship that sounded pretty DOA if you asked me. He continued on about how hard it was to date while being in the funeral-directing field because of the continual on call and long working hours lifestyle.

"My ideal girlfriend is someone in the field so that she understands the demands of the job without being disappointed when I have to leave our date suddenly or change our plans." He looked defeated. "I didn't realize what I had when I had it, and now that I see that, I want us back. I still love you."

Did he genuinely love me and want me back, or was he tired of being turned down and know that I would always take him back? He was becoming so much more mature than he had been in school. I was impressed with him as a whole on this trip, but I had to convince myself that it wasn't enough. I needed to go back to my new home, eight hundred miles away from him.

26

The Mind Has A Heart of Its Own

I hung out with Jordan and his friends a few more times, and I was noticing that it was really hard to be friends only. I was so impressed by this guy and the way he carried himself. I loved being with him and I loved who I was when I was around him, but it felt different. It wasn't nervous excitement when I got ready to see him. Sure, there were butterflies, but it was just pure joy. It was effortless to have a great time with him. I was so at ease and peaceful. I liked how I felt with him.

I was worried about these feelings though because the

last thing I wanted was to be in a relationship. I kind of blamed him for making me like him so much. I wanted to be single and just make some new friends. I was not looking for a boyfriend, and in fact, I was fighting it, especially when he would ask me about friends from home and my recent time in college. I remembered it as the best year of my life. I told him about my actual hometown and how I decided to move to the city for school and how I then got recruited to New York. He was so surprised that I didn't have any family or friends out here and that I would just up and move to a totally unfamiliar place. He said he admired that about me— the bravery and confidence it would take to do that. I didn't tell him all of the details of my decision making of course. It was too new to bring up ex-boyfriend baggage. I wasn't going to shed the compliment by saying that I was just trying to run far away from my ex to prevent myself from going back to him for the fiftieth time. I talked about my group of college friends and lumped Evan in there also, which was the truth. He and I were still friends and kept in touch through group chats, texts, phone calls and social media.

As I found myself slipping into the beginning stages of a relationship with Jordan, I couldn't help but reminisce about my time with Evan. They had so many physical similarities— the same clothes, the same hobbies and interests, and so on. I couldn't help but think, *I've been on a date with this blue-striped shirt before*, or *I know all about that basketball team you just mentioned because Evan told me all about them*. But none of that matters in a relationship. What mattered most was how they were different. Jordan wasn't jealous or possessive. It was so different than what I was used to. Evan would get jealous if I was polite to the cashier at the grocery store, whereas Jordan encouraged me to talk with his guy friends and get to know his whole friend group.

I wanted to move on, and I really was doing a great job at it. I barely thought about Evan anymore, especially when I was with Jordan. The problem with Evan was that I tended to remember him at his best and us at our worst. I was feeling good with the excitement of a new relationship. It was off to a great start, and I was feeling very pampered and well taken care of, as if my heart was finally protected, but I still couldn't help but hear Evan in my head saying, "I give it three weeks," like he had said before. I felt my confidence shake like an earthquake hit it, and then my mind wandered. Would it only last a short while? Would I go back to Evan in the end? I thought about the mornings when Evan would hear me rustling awake so he'd head back into the dark room where only a little bit of sunlight was peeking through his blinds, with a beaming grin on his face and more energy than I could think to muster in that morning. He'd take a running leap from the doorway toward his bed and land right on top of me before smothering me in obnoxious kisses through the blankets I pulled over my head. "Stop!" I'd squeal through my laughter.

"It's time to get up. I made you coffee," he'd say enticingly.

If it wasn't a flying leap of smothering kisses, it was a tired roll-over of bear hugs from behind or pulling me into his chest as if to protect me from the morning. These types of mornings, I wanted anything but to be protected from. I dreamed of them, I missed them, and I craved them. I shook my head and focused on where I was and what I had. Maybe when Jordan and I spent the night together, we'd make memories like those. What if they were better? I could possibly feel that same joy and not worry that we'd be a mess hours later. I wasn't in any hurry to be spending the night with anyone new though. I needed to wait until those flashbacks and comparisons stopped. I wasn't going to move on with someone new until Evan was out of my head.

My first date with Jordan was wonderful. He took me to the actual oldest mini golf course in America, and then we went to a nearby spot to have drinks on the beach and watch the sunset. He knew me so well already because that date was perfect and exactly what I would have planned myself. I was beaming even though he kicked my competitive butt in mini golf. This guy's commentary is out of this world. His dry sense of humor would get him far, especially with me. If I remember right, he named me "Nelloser" on my scorecard, and banter like that was a sure way to get my attention. The weather was perfect as we sat on the beach to watch the sunset. It was a small bar, so small that you had to sit outside in the sand—not that anyone would want to sit inside with a view like that. It was lake as far as the eye could see, and the orange tones of the sunset made for a nice, romantic evening.

Jordan was a true gentleman and didn't push his luck for a first-date kiss. In fact, every relationship milestone moved slowly with Jordan. I was learning that he is an incredibly patient man. I found myself wondering if we were teetering on the ledge of just friends and a romantic connection. I called Kelsey and Taylor and asked for their opinion on what they thought our relationship was or could be if we were moving at a snail's pace like that. "He likes me, right? How long did you wait for your first kiss?" I asked them.

"He's into men, Nellie," Taylor said as if that were the only way to explain it.

"No way, Taylor," Kelsey said sternly. "He's just a

gentleman. I know that's out of your wheelhouse, Taylor, but some guys have manners."

She had a point. I didn't rule out his interest in me. He was just taking his time, whereas Evan ran straight to home plate the second he could. When we finally shared our first kiss, it was worth the wait. It wasn't a moment that knocked me off my feet, but it certainly caught me off guard. I think he had finally reached his boiling point when he couldn't wait anymore because as I was leaving his house one day, he grabbed my arm to pull me back and gently kissed me. It was gentle enough to feel soft and airy, but afterward, I noticed my back was to the wall. He had a finesse with me that I wasn't familiar with. He didn't push me into the wall or grab my arm in an urgent way. As he grabbed my arm, his grip was so soft that his hand was in my hand by the time our lips touched. It was all so delicate but still made my heart skip. I had the same smile on my face from the end of the kiss until I got halfway home.

27

Good Bones

I was raised Christian, therefore as a nod to my values, I was very interested in a good ol' church-going boy to make Grandma proud. I perked up when a guy mentioned his church upbringing, like a reflex to the topic. So, when Jordan mentioned he attended Catholic school growing up, I swooned. He clarified that he no longer believed in the religion and found religion to be a negative in his life, yet he lived out all of the qualities of a believer. He was patient, he was loving, and he was kind. He didn't boast, he wasn't greedy, and he seemed very forgiving. How could someone who had all those qualities have such a negative feeling toward the upbringing that taught him all of that? I didn't want it to be a deal breaker that he refused to go to church with me. He was allowed to be his own person, but I really did want that for my future. I always imagined taking my kids and husband to church on Sunday, maybe even walking there and then going out to breakfast together right afterward. It was an image of how I saw my future. He seemed pretty firm that that wasn't a vision he had of his future. I would be lying if I said this wasn't a red flag in our relationship. I didn't go to church every Sunday, but part of me wanted someone to encourage me to, someone to teach our kids how to pray before they ate. It didn't seem like Jordan fit this ideal. This was the only red flag so far, so I let it slide and appreciated his actions of Christianity, which certainly spoke louder than his words.

I noticed that life as a whole was a lot simpler now. There was less chaos around me and fewer hurdles to overcome. Did it have something to do with this new peaceful lifestyle of mine, or was it simply that I was becoming more settled and surrounding myself with more mature people? I chalked it up to being because of this new peaceful state of mind our relationship put me in. There was nothing interesting or edge-of-your-seat captivating about our relationship. It was calm, it was easy, and it was reliable. He didn't throw me against a wall while making out with me, nor had he ripped off any of my clothing in an effort to get me naked within seconds. But he was my biggest supporter and my best friend in New York. When something good happened, he was the first person I wanted to tell so that we could celebrate together. When something bad happened, he was the hug I wanted to run to and the one who would ease my mind and talk me back to a calm state. He was softly handsome, so I hadn't grown tired of looking at him. Would the ease and serenity be enough to keep my attention though? Clearly, I was attracted to chaos, right?

I made him wait and took my time, mainly because I wasn't ready to date but also because I wanted to turn a healthy relationship leaf and really take my time into it all. I flashed back multiple times to my conversation with Justin, one of my friends from college, during one of our therapeutic runs in the woods. We did that a few times throughout our year in school and he was so patient with me. He was a marathon runner and could easily triple my speed and stamina without getting winded, yet I was sweating and panting and taking long breaks in between words trying to carry on a conversation even though he had slowed way down to match my pace. After a while, we stopped running because I felt badly for holding him back. I knew his crazy schedule because it mimicked mine. Running was an outlet for him, and my urge to please people made me feel guilty for holding him back during our runs even though we had such a great time on them. We had even switched it up occasionally and rode our bikes, which I was much better at, on the trails until it got too cold. One time, it had rained so much that there were puddles deep enough in some spots that it covered half of the wheels of our bikes. Our ankles were fully submerged in water at times, but it didn't stop us. We pedaled through the water and continued talking once the absurd obstacle was behind us. On these runs and bike rides, we talked about so many things that were either bothering us or getting us through our crazy schedules. He coached me through my heartbreaks with Evan and gave me advice on how to move forward with him even though it was against his will at times. He was one of the many friends who thought Evan and I would be better off apart than together.

He knew I loved him, and he knew that Evan loved me because he was Evan's friend too, and they would talk just as much as he and I did. Justin was an accidental middleman to my and Evan's relationship. He told me that love shouldn't hurt as much as our relationship did. He also said that he hadn't met another two people crazier about each other. I was getting mixed reviews from friends from day one, so his contradicting statements didn't faze me either. It felt like no one knew how to handle what Evan and I had. No one could give me genuine advice on the matter because no one knew the whole story of any stage of our relationship. Justin would tell me that even though he knew how much we cared about each other and wanted to be together, that he thought I deserved better. As a dear friend, he knew that Evan made me happy, but he felt I could be happier with someone who took better care of me. He was right, but in the moment, it didn't feel right. It didn't make sense to me that Evan wouldn't be the one for me. I couldn't stomach the idea of him ending up with someone else. In fact, it angered me to think that after all of the pain I went through with him that it wasn't all for something, that I wasn't going to get to wake up one day to everything being easier and steadier. I couldn't imagine dealing with a relationship as chaotic as ours every day, but even more than that, I couldn't imagine letting it go. Justin promised me that one day I would feel okay with either letting him go or fighting through the chaos every day and that one day we'd make the decision together and be on the same page. I was still waiting for this part.

He brought up a good point that since Evan and I had moved so quickly in the beginning of our relationship that we started off our axis. He told me to make a promise to myself that if there was to be a relationship after Evan, I needed to wait a very long time before kissing the guy, before sleeping with him, and especially before telling him I loved him. He clarified that the wait would weed out any of the boys and leave the deserving men standing clear.

I thought back to this moment a lot in the beginning of my relationship with Jordan. We waited months upon months before sleeping together. It was such a long wait that I was starting to wonder if maybe he had an erectile dysfunction issue, or maybe we were just friends. I'm by no means one to rush someone to take additional steps before they're ready. I never said anything to him to insinuate that I was antsy or eager, and I never once asked him why we were waiting so long. He waited seven months to tell me he loved me, and I waited another month before I said it back. I felt it but I couldn't say it out loud, so most of the time, I would smile after he professed his love for me or pretend like I didn't hear him. I even went in for a kiss to fill the air without saying it back. Again, it was not that I didn't love him, because I did, but it had been a while since I had said that to a guy, and it meant a lot to me to say it again.

28

What I Need

There was also a certain comfort about Jordan in the beginning that convinced me I no longer wanted to stay single and wanted to be with him. We started off very slowly and kept that slow pace throughout our relationship. There wasn't any urgency behind any of it. With Evan, I was impatient and overwhelmed with passion, but with Jordan, I was calmer and steadier but in no way uninterested.

Jordan and I were very different people with different perspectives on certain topics, different routines, and especially different opinions on home decor and function. Bless his sweet heart, but I would be taking over the decorating if we moved in together. Please and thank you. Most guys didn't notice when you changed the color of the curtains, added a new rug, or, heck, even changed out the furniture, but this guy noticed if I turned a table lamp three degrees to the right. He'd sternly tell me to please move it back the way it was.

Trying to convince him that the vomit-green color in his bedroom wasn't inviting and should probably be painted over was like trying to run in nine feet of water—impossible, pointless, and made you kind of look like a fool for trying. Through all of his weird quirks and Jordan-isms, he was so sure of himself and confident in a refreshing, not arrogant, way. It was more charming. He made me want to be more like that. He was so unapologetically himself and knew what he liked and disliked. I loved this about him. I also loved that he didn't get jealous and genuinely trusted me. So, breaking the news to him that I was still good friends with my ex didn't faze him a bit. He was so shockingly calm about it that I wondered if he was in fact made of robot parts. Any other guy I knew would have hated hearing that, but not this guy. Also, he had nothing to worry about, and I'm sure he knew that. I was in a great place with Evan. I felt that we had found our friend niche. Jordan and I had really gotten into a routine and were a powerhouse couple. He bettered me and I, him. I really could see a future with this guy, and I wanted it. He was my other red-string love. My peaceful, easy love. I could get used to this easy, peaceful love. He was the person I loved to do everyday tasks with. Tasks that would seem mundane were enjoyable with him. Sure, we went on nice dates and trips together, but they were never extravagant, and I loved every second. When you can genuinely say that you're having the best day when it's the two of you running errands together, that's what really matters. "Marry the person you love to do everyday things with" was written on a canvas wall-hanging that I saw when I was out shopping, and I thought to myself, *Okay, I will.*

29

My Turn

I should have known that you literally cannot have your cake and eat it too.

After a few years of bliss, Evan called, but this wasn't rare. We talked on the phone occasionally, just about life and its highs and lows. This phone call was different though. He told me that he bought a house and that his closing date was in a few months. I was so happy for him, a jealous happy because I felt a little bummed that I couldn't be there to celebrate with him as he took this big adult step. Before I could finish my congratulatory statement, he cut me off and continued, "It's a fixer-upper like you said you wanted on that first day of school."

"What?" I was certain he was planning to follow that up with a poorly structured joke.

"It's a great location, right by the funeral home. I could see our kids playing in the backyard. There's even a spot for your garden."

I was nothing short of silent.

"I'll take care of you financially until you get into a routine and a job out here. I can do that. I want to take care of you."

I didn't believe what I was hearing. I didn't know what to say back. I was so angry that he chose this moment to offer me everything I had wanted and fought so hard for while he and I were together. Should I run back into the arms of the guy who knew how to sweep me off my feet with just a wink? I had the chance to dance with him in the kitchen for years to come. I was offered the chance to lie next to him as he ran his fingers through my hair to wake me up in the morning. He was my dearest friend and kryptonite all at the same time. How could I possibly walk away from him when he had offered me exactly what I'd been asking for from him? I needed to reply to him in some way, but I couldn't catch my breath or come up with anything to say. The last few years of my life just kept replaying in my head, and I felt the love and the heartache, the good and the bad, all over again. It was as if I had just finished running a marathon and crossed the finish line in last place with my hands on my knees and my head hanging low.

This phone call had come out of nowhere, and I wasn't ready. "I have to go," was all I could say before I hung up the phone. Just as he had left me hanging at my proposal to take a leap, it was my turn to say nothing in return. I couldn't help but reflect on the time I had offered to take the job near him and continue our relationship side by side, and he had said nothing to me, he just got up and left.

I had the life I had always prayed for, and the future I had always wished for was actually visible and within reach. This was where I belonged, with Jordan in the life we were building together. I knew that. But even when you've been eating healthy and living your best life, if someone offers you a warm chocolate cake with a scoop of melty ice cream on top, you think about it. You can taste the chocolate and feel the warm mixing with the cool in your mouth. Even though you turn it down, it sounded good for a second.

30

Can I?

The difference between the two was that I was made for Evan, and Jordan was made for me. I was meant to show Evan what genuine love was like, what it felt like to have someone in your life who would love you and continue to even when you mess up—unconditionally. Through all the craziness, I was there for him anytime he needed or wanted me.

Jordan was made for me to finally give me the love I deserved and that I'd been giving to others and never receiving in return. He showed me what true love felt like.

I'm grateful for them both and wouldn't change a thing

about the journey or the pain. It taught me a lot about love and myself, especially how to love myself.

If it wasn't for Evan breaking my heart in a way that I couldn't repair unless I knew I wouldn't have to cross his path but once a year, and if I hadn't moved states away after taking the option alternate to the one he'd shut down so fiercely, I wouldn't have the life I have now. I wouldn't have met Jordan. I had Evan to thank for that. I thanked him for the memories of the good and the outcome of the bad. I looked at him with grateful eyes and vowed to remember him as the guy who made my heart flutter in a cafeteria the first time I saw him and as the guy who held me so tenderly as he kissed me under the light of the city against the black sky. I spent so much time telling myself that I would always love him and never allow myself to ever again be *in love* with him. Could I keep this promise to myself? Should I even keep this promise to myself? I had a huge decision to make.

31

Wave Break

I asked for the window seat, like I usually do because I like to look out at the land as I fly over it. There's something about seeing it all as a whole that makes traveling even more exciting. This time was especially exciting because I hadn't yet flown this far out over the water before. I wanted to see the contrast in the color from the varying depths of the ocean. I was so relaxed looking out the window and seeing nothing but shades of blue.

I had a plastic cup of overpriced gin and tonic in my left hand. I periodically let go of the cup to admire the beautiful diamond ring on my ring finger. I couldn't help but beam with joy when I looked at it. It symbolized so much—love, determination, and excitement. I had my custom-made, white wedding dress in my carry-on because I knew better than to let it out of my sight. My bags were packed full of sundresses, swimsuits, and sandals. I was ready for these ten days in paradise with my fiancé, my soon-to-be husband. I couldn't believe those words—*fiancé* and *husband*! I knew what I wanted, and I was going for it. All in.

He and I decided to elope to St. Thomas, just the two of us—no family and no friends. He wanted a memorable vacation in paradise with just the two of us celebrating our love for one another, and I was all for it. I could just picture myself saying, "I do," with my feet in the sand and a subtle sunburn beginning on the tips of my shoulders. I had been thinking about this for a while now, and it was coming to fruition.

We landed in St. Thomas and were both smitten by the palm trees and atmosphere of relaxation. We rented our convertible car and headed to the resort, which was sheer luxury. There were rows of canopies overlooking the water, one of which would soon be ours for the day. It felt great to belly flop into the bright-white comforter on the bed as he rolled our bags into our honeymoon suite. I was surprised by the thickness of the comforter in paradise until I realized the air conditioner was blasting in our room on high. I sat up and hopped off the bed as I heard my fiancé shout to me to join him on the balcony. The view was breathtaking, and the breeze was heavenly, just soft enough to cool us off as we began to feel warm—almost as if the air did not even exist. We didn't feel hot or chilly. There was no temperature. It was just purely perfect. He wrapped his arms around my waist to pull me into him, and whispered to me how much he loved me, us together, and that we were getting married.

We got acclimated to the area as we searched for a place for dinner, picked up our marriage license, and chatted with the concierge when we picked up our wedding gifts that were called into the resort for us by our friends. She recommended a list of places we had to check out while we were on the island. We looked over the list as we enjoyed our gifted champagne, fruit platters & fresh local flowers. All of the activities sounded enticing but there was one activity we were most excited for- our wedding.

As I was getting ready to walk down my sandy aisle, I started to tear up with joy. I couldn't believe where life had taken me and how I had gotten to this point to deserve such a beautiful moment. The ukulele player began, and I looked up to see *him* standing at the edge of where the water met the sand. My soon-to-be husband was about twenty yards from me, but I felt his euphoria from where I was standing. I couldn't help but tear up even more because when he first saw me, he beamed with happiness and looked down at the sand in front of him while he laughed with joy and then looked back up to me with those loving eyes. I walked toward him with the sun glowing on me and the breeze delicately blowing my hair and dress. I walked toward my soon-to-be husband and the breathtaking ocean.

"Do you, Penelope Cooper, promise that through sickness and health, for richer or poorer, you will love this willing man unconditionally? Do you promise to share your life together in full commitment and love for one another no matter the circumstances? Do you vow to put him above all others and cherish your future together, until death do you part?"

"I do."

About the Author

Lainey Schmidt hasn't even reached her thirties yet and has already lived what many call "the most interesting life". That doesn't come without poor decisions or great memories.

Her debut book is about the chaos we all go through while dating and falling in love, or trying to at least. A topic she knows a lot about having lived it and learned it from her friends experiencing it along with her. She's known for her honesty, quick wit and willingness to jump in feet first. When someone like that puts her thoughts to paper, it creates a story worth sharing.

This upstate New Yorker has a lot to say and plenty of pages to say it on. Lainey's personality shines throughout this book, giving the reader a story they can relate to.

Printed in the United States
By Bookmasters